# Nantucket Solstice

## A Nantucket Sunset Series

## Katie Winters

# Chapter One

The letter came out of nowhere with no return address. It was addressed to Greta. She found it on the kitchen table at a quarter past four when she was busy making a snack for her grandson James and his troupe of high school friends—all of whom had appetites like mountain lions and appreciated Greta's cooking more than anyone. With the homemade mozzarella sticks in the oven and a guacamole and hummus dip on the counter, she washed her hands and inspected the letter further. It just said her name and "The Copperfield House." It was suspicious and just the sort of mystery Greta craved.

Greta reached for a knife to tear open the envelope just as her eldest daughter, Alana, entered the kitchen. At nearly forty-seven, Alana was still the most beautiful woman Greta had ever seen, and she seemed to become happier and more graceful by the day. Greta had been a pretty younger woman but never a knock-out like Alana. But Greta had long felt that Alana's beauty had been more a curse than anything. Alana had worked as a model for many years, but those years had dried up as soon as she'd hit the latter part of her twenties. And her acting career had disintegrated after a few commercials. Greta was a writer. She liked to sit in rooms alone and rely on her intellect. This was part of the reason she could never fully understand Alana and part of the reason why she pitied her.

But Alana didn't look pitiable right now. "I'm so nervous about later," Alana said. She opened the fridge and sighed as she searched the compartments for a snack. She closed it a few seconds later.

"It's going to be great," Greta assured her. "I know what a brilliant cook you are."

"Yeah. Right." Alana rolled her eyes and sniffed. "What are you making, anyway?"

Greta told her.

"James is so spoiled," Alana teased.

"You were spoiled, too," Greta reminded her. "And you know I'll make you homemade mozzarella sticks whenever you want. Just because you're moving in with Jeremy doesn't mean you aren't welcome here."

"Thank you for saying that." Alana laughed and pulled her hair into a ponytail. "The girls should be here soon. I'd better get up there."

Alana hosted an acting school for teenage girls at The Copperfield House. It was remarkable to watch her mold teenage girls, build their confidence, and help them fall in love with theater. Alana didn't have children of her own, but she called all her students her "kids." Greta knew how much it meant to her. Alana had also been instrumental in helping them accept and love their bodies, which was a difficult feat during their teenage years. That was how she'd initially met her boyfriend Jeremy's daughter, Sarah. Sarah had struggled with anorexia, whittling herself down to eighty or ninety pounds. Jeremy hadn't known what to do. However, Alana's background in modeling and her revaluation of what matters in life had been a masterclass in helping Sarah get through the darkest period in her young life.

"What's that?" Alana asked about the envelope in Greta's hand. She was poised in the doorway.

"Just a bill," Greta lied.

Alana disappeared upstairs and left Greta to stew in the stupidity of her lie. Why hadn't she told Alana she didn't know? Why did she want to hide this? Who did she think it was from? The handwriting could have been anyone's, male or female. She racked her memories for clues but found nothing. In her life, she'd only had two real loves—one of whom she'd married and the other of whom never wanted to see her again (and vice versa). That meant the letter was probably from an old friend.

Greta shivered as she tore open the envelope and removed the letter.

Immediately, she had to sit down.

The letter was from Celeste Harding.

*Greta,*

*It has been too long. I hate that it's been so long. I think of a poet we both adored, Maya Angelou and the poem she wrote about friendship. About how none of us will make it in this world alone.*

*I think about our year of loneliness in Nantucket. I often reflect on it and wonder how you are and if you ever found your path away from loneliness.*

*I will be in Nantucket mid-May. I would love to meet you. Find my phone number written at the end of this letter. Only write me if you feel up to it. I will not bother you otherwise.*

*Yours,*

*Celeste*

The beeper sounded on the oven, and Greta burst up to remove the mozzarella sticks. The front door of The Copperfield House screamed open to bring in six teenage boys—James and his friends—and they ambled into the kitchen for snacks and sodas. Greta touched James' head and mussed his hair as they breezed back out.

"How was school?" Greta asked, feeling like she'd had the wind knocked out of her. "How are you?"

"We're good, Grandma. Thank you for the food," James said as he led his friends to the back patio. A few seconds later came the sound of the speaker they always carried around. It was music Greta now recognized—rap and hip hop—and nothing she would have ever picked for herself. But it warmed her heart, as ever, that The Copperfield House was bustling again.

Celeste had lived here for a little more than a year. If Greta wasn't mistaken, it was between May 2003 and November 2004—six years after Bernard Copperfield had been taken to prison and a few years after Ella had left the nest. Greta had been like a ghost haunting The Copperfield House. She'd hardly gotten dressed and meandered from one floor to the next, reading and playing the piano and hardly ever putting pen to paper or her fingers on her keyboard. She felt dried-up. Sadder than any woman in the world. And that's when Celeste had darkened her door.

With James on the patio and a few hours left before

she had to leave for Alana and Jeremy's, Greta hurried upstairs to google Celeste. It amazed her she hadn't considered doing this before. She'd always told Celeste, "You're the most talented person to ever enter The Copperfield House. You're on your way somewhere. Mark my words." But she hadn't heard Celeste's name anywhere, hadn't read it on any theatre blogs, hadn't heard it whispered in the literary circles she and Bernard had recently rejoined. It struck her as bizarre.

More bizarre was the fact that Celeste's name hardly came up on google. There was one photograph of Celeste at the age of twenty-five—a couple of years after her stay at The Copperfield House. In the image she wore a black dress with spaghetti straps and stood off to the right of a theatre stage. This was probably where she'd worked after she'd embarked on a trip to the big city after her stay at The Copperfield House. But what happened afterward?

Greta was stumped.

What had happened to Celeste? Why hadn't she had the career of her dreams?

Bernard knocked gently on Greta's office door and entered when Greta gave the okay. Greta spun around in her office chair and blinked at him through the darkness. The afternoon light had dimmed to grays and purples, but she'd been too distracted to turn on the overhead light.

"Are you about ready to go?" Bernard asked.

Greta flinched and jumped up from the chair. "What time is it?"

"We have to leave in about fifteen minutes," Bernard said.

Greta tugged her hair and flew past him en route to their bedroom. "I just have to put on fresh clothes!"

She could hear her husband chuckling behind her. He knew what she was like when she got "lost" in a writing project. But this time, she hadn't been lost in a novel. She'd been lost in the throes of her memories, trying to make sense of the year and four months she'd spent with Celeste and what might have gone wrong after she'd left. Bernard didn't know anything about Celeste, nor did any of her children. It was difficult to verbalize the truth that Celeste had been Greta's stand-in family when hers had abandoned her.

Sometimes, it was still difficult not to feel angry about all the time that had been taken from her. A therapist had suggested those feelings would eb and flow forever, no matter how often she focused on forgiveness. And with this letter from Celeste, these feelings had come back with a vengeance.

It begged the question of whether she wanted to see Celeste at all when she came in mid-May. Or would it be too painful?

Greta put on a pair of slacks and a blouse, fluffed her hair, put on a dark red shade of lipstick, and cut back downstairs to join Bernard in his car. The walk to Jeremy's place took less than twenty minutes, but it was still early May on Nantucket, which meant frigid temperatures when it got too late. On the way to the dinner party, Bernard asked Greta questions about his current manuscript. Greta had read it numerous times already and could give him tips.

"Do you think a character like that would actually do something that reckless?" he asked, second-guessing his characters' intentions. "Do you actually think a man who grew up in Wisconsin would say something like that?"

Greta answered as best as she could and touched his thigh. This was part of the reason they'd fallen in love in the first place; they'd both been the most brilliant and creative person they'd ever met, and they didn't want their conversations to stop. Not ever. And now that Bernard was home, they could do it for the rest of time.

It had been more than two years since he'd returned. The change had given her a form of whiplash that she wasn't sure she would ever recover from.

Jeremy lived in a two-story house with his newly graduated daughter Sarah and, as of recently, Alana. The house had light blue shutters and fir trees outside, and it came with a pool in the back, which Alana had promised was open to all Copperfields who wanted to swim in it as soon as it got warm enough. (Greta wasn't sure why you would ever swim in a pool when the Nantucket Sound was right there but to each his own.) Bernard and Greta were the last to arrive. Julia's SUV was parked along the road; Quentin's fancy sports car was in the driveway; Ella and Will's junky van was behind it, and other second-hand cars that belonged to the teenagers in the family were scattered about. It was Alana's first "family party" in her own place, and the air bubbled with curiosity. It was strange to pull all of the Copperfields away from The Copperfield House.

Alana opened the door wearing an apron. Her cheeks were cherry red from the heat of her oven and stove top. "Welcome! We were wondering what happened to you."

"We're not that late!" Greta laughed and hugged Alana. "How is the cooking going? Do you need any help?"

"Julia came in the nick of time," Alana said. "Come on. I'll pour you some wine."

Greta had only been in Jeremy's house one other time and only briefly, but that didn't matter anyway, as Alana had completely changed it. It was cozy but slightly strange and colorful, and it was completely Alana. "What do you think of it?" Alana asked. "I realized I hadn't made any decorating decisions since Paris. And in Paris, your house has to look a certain way if you want to fit in with certain crowds." She rolled her eyes as she poured Greta a glass of red. "I just wanted to lean into whatever decorations I really wanted. I said yes to whatever colors spoke to my heart."

Jeremy strode into the kitchen and shook Bernard's hand. He looked every bit the all-American jock he'd been at eighteen—handsome and formidable and strong. When he looked at Alana, you could see the immensity of their love. Sometimes it amazed Greta that Alana had been all over the world, worked so many different jobs and met so many different types of people, and still, she wanted to get back together with her high school jock boyfriend. But nothing got in the way of true love.

"How's the first week going?" Bernard asked with a wry laugh.

"No big fights yet," Alana joked. "And Sarah might be on her way to the city, so we might have the house to ourselves for the summer."

Greta brightened. "Is she going to audition for that play?"

Alana clasped her hands together and beamed. "It took some convincing. But she's good, Mom. Really good. I think she could be something."

Jeremy rubbed his temples and gave Bernard a look.

"I'm terrified, Bernard. I don't want my only daughter running off to the big city. She's barely nineteen, for crying out loud."

"I know. But you have to let your kids explore their passions," Bernard said, clapping his shoulder.

"It's awful," Jeremy said with a laugh. "Nobody tells you it will be this hard to let them go."

Greta and Bernard joined the others at the big dinner table. Greta was seated between her darling son Quentin and her granddaughter Scarlet Copperfield. Scarlet squeezed her hand under the table as Alana and Julia piled the table with dishes containing roasted lamb, buttery potatoes, beans, several different types of salad, and more bottles of wine. She watched Alana like a hawk, wondering what it was like for her to slip into this care-taker role for the first time. Greta knew a great deal about Alana's life before The Copperfield House—a time when she'd been married to an extremely handsome, rich, and successful artist who'd made them a great deal of money and, of course, broken her heart. Everything had been done for Alana. She'd never had to clean a toilet in her life.

"Before we get started," Jeremy began, still standing behind his chair with his wine glass raised, "Alana and I want to make an announcement." Jeremy smiled at Alana adorably as she came toward him and wrapped her arm around his waist. They made eye contact and laughed nervously.

"Get on with it!" Quentin teased, raising his glass.

Alana stuck her tongue out at him and burst into giggles. "We're getting married," Alana said finally, wrapping a curl around her ear.

Greta was on her feet in a flash. She rushed around

the table and threw her arms around Alana. This was the daughter she'd never fully understood and, therefore, the daughter she worried about the most. The fact that Alana had found her happily ever after with someone good, someone besides Asher, someone on Nantucket Island, thrilled her to the bone. Julia and Ella were there, too, and they peppered Alana with questions. The food had been abandoned.

"Soon!" Alana explained. "We want to do it at the end of July or something. And we were hoping we could have it at The Copperfield House?" She winced as she asked.

"Of course!" Greta cried. "It's the perfect place for it."

It blew her mind that Alana, of all her children, wanted a wedding at The Copperfield House. Alana was the most interested in elegance and finery, and there were certainly many hotels and wedding venues across Nantucket—ones that would suit her disposition. But perhaps this was proof that Alana fully accepted her status as a Copperfield. Perhaps it was proof that she felt she fully belonged.

Eventually, they returned to their seats, but the conversation and questions didn't let up for a second. Alana and Jeremy often held hands over the tabletop. Jeremy gushed with excitement, and even his daughter, Sarah, offered her two cents. "Alana already feels like a part of our family."

"Sarah promised to write a speech for our wedding," Alana said tenderly.

Sarah laughed and blushed. "Don't build up too much excitement. I don't want to disappoint."

"You won't, honey," Julia assured her. "I've seen you on stage. You have such amazing stage presence."

"Nobody said I was a writer, though," Sarah said. "There are already so many writers in the Copperfield family!"

"We always welcome more," Greta said.

They fell into a beautiful celebration. After dinner, Greta helped her daughters clean the table and served apple pie on the back porch, where they watched a big yellow sun drop into the pink ocean. Greta felt in her pocket for the letter from Celeste, which she'd packed with her for reasons she didn't remember. She wondered where Celeste was living now and why she hadn't included the return address on the envelope. Was she in danger? Is that why she was coming back?

It was true that when Celeste had left in 2004, Greta had fallen into the darkest of depressions. She'd fallen so deep that she hadn't recognized herself for years after that. Maybe she hadn't even fully recognized herself until the summer her children had come home to save her. She'd carried a Celeste-sized hole in her heart.

Greta excused herself for the bathroom and removed her letter from her pocket. Celeste had written her phone number clear as anything on the bottom. Greta took a breath and typed it out.

GRETA: Celeste, I got your letter. It's Greta.

GRETA: I would love to see you when you come to Nantucket.

GRETA: I can't wait to catch up.

Greta looked at her phone for a few minutes, waiting

for a response. But the text from Celeste didn't come till the following day.

CELESTE: Wonderful. Let's meet at that French café you always liked. May 14th at three in the afternoon?

GRETA: Perfect. I'll see you there.

# Chapter Two

Sarah's audition in New York City was set for the morning of May 14th, which meant she needed to get down to the city the day before. Jeremy couldn't get off work at the Nantucket Records' Office to take her, but Sarah confessed to Alana privately that she didn't want him to go anyway. "You understand this world, Alana," Sarah said. "Dad just doesn't. He would never want to leave Nantucket. And he definitely doesn't want me to go."

Alana hesitated and filled her mouth with coffee. The May morning was splendorous, with a blue sky speckled with fluffy white clouds. She tried to put herself in Sarah's shoes, to remember exactly what it had been like to throw herself into her career of being "seen" in fabulous and very expensive cities filled with judgemental people. She hadn't thought Greta and Bernard understood her, either. But they'd known far more than she'd given them credit for back then. That was the nature of being a teenager.

"Your dad wanted to go away for college, remember?" Alana said with a smile.

"He wanted to move to Indiana to play football. That's different."

"It was Notre Dame football," Alana corrected. "That's some of the best football in the league."

Sarah pulled her long hair into a ponytail and looked out the window. Her face was sour. Alana thought for a moment she'd lost her respect. It was always difficult with teenagers. One minute, you were on their good side; the next minute, all was lost.

But then Sarah said, "I'm sorry. I'm acting like a brat because I'm nervous."

Alana reminded her just how ready she was. They'd been running Sarah's lines for months, so much so that Jeremy had asked for a moratorium on theater at the dinner table. They often walked the beach as Alana read the lines of every other character who interacted with the character Sarah wanted to portray. Alana now felt that the play was stitched into the back of her own mind. Perhaps she could have done a one-woman show and played all the parts.

But her acting days were over. And she'd promised to throw all of her energy into ensuring Sarah had a wonderful career. But for Alana, that meant protecting Sarah. Alana had been thrown to the wolves' time and time again. Being famous hadn't done her many favors. She hoped that if Sarah got off on the right foot, she could protect herself from future predators. She could be stronger than Alana ever was.

Alana drove Sarah to the Nantucket Port, where they boarded the ferry and set out for their Manhattan adventure. Sarah took a selfie of the two of them on the top deck of the boat and captioned it: **On my way to Manhattan! Wish me luck!**

Alana took a picture of them, too, but didn't post it anywhere. She liked to keep her memories to herself.

"Everyone says that you have to build a social platform if you want to be anyone these days," Sarah explained as they slipped back into Alana's car. "People have to already know who you are if they hire you for performances and films and stuff."

"That sounds exhausting," Alana said. Putting yourself at the mercy of an audience was enough of a task. Knowing that the entire internet could also watch your every move was terrifying.

"You were just discovered from a painting, right?" Sarah asked.

Alana wrinkled her nose at the memory. It was true that Asher's painting of her had launched her modeling career—and her romantic life. It had taken her away from Nantucket and into the traumatic horrors of fame. But she was still grateful she hadn't had to curate a social media presence. At the rate she'd partied in her twenties, it was unlikely her social media presence would have been coherent, anyway. She'd probably have launched a few scandals.

Alana and Sarah reached their Midtown hotel at a quarter past three and parked in the below-ground parking garage. Their hotel room was quaint with a single room, two double beds, a large television, and a coffee maker. Sarah set down her bag and went to the window to look at the view all the way down Fifth Avenue. Alana's heart thumped. She watched Sarah's expression, knowing that it was filled with optimism and endless hope. If Sarah didn't get this gig, she would be heartbroken. But the odds were always against actresses. There were just so many of them. So many beautiful, talented girls whose hearts were on the verge of breaking.

"Let's go out on the town!" Alana suggested.

They changed into dresses and jackets and stepped outside into the thrumming chaos of the biggest city either of them had ever known. Before long, they were shopping, hopping in and out of little boutiques and vintage places, looking through swimsuits for the approaching summer season, buying ice cream and licking it as they ran around. For these blissful hours, Sarah seemed to forget her nerves for tomorrow's audition. This meant that Alana was doing her job right.

Just before seven Alana announced she had a surprise. "Follow me," she said as she ducked into the Empire State Building.

Sarah walloped with laughter and ran after her. Alana removed her phone to retrieve the tickets she'd preordered for the top of the Empire State Building. They bypassed the line that wove through the bottom floor and out onto the sidewalk. They went up and up in the elevator, and Sarah squeezed her hand. Alana wondered what it would have been like to raise Sarah from girlhood. She loved her so tremendously after only two years of knowing her. Alana imagined that a lifetime of love would have killed her. It would have been too much.

They stepped into the caged enclosure at the top of the Empire State Building and went immediately to the bars to peer north. They were wordless. Most everyone else this far up was quiet, too. There was just something sensational about being so far above a city of millions. You genuinely felt so small, like your little life didn't matter so much, and all your endless fears and worries were for nothing.

"You won't take my baby," Sarah breathed through the bars. "I won't let you."

A shiver went down Alana's spine. This was one of Sarah's character's first lines in the play. She wanted to run lines for her audition. And she wanted to do them dramatically here above the city.

"You know you aren't ready for something like this," Alana returned the lines of the character's father. "You'll be back in the institution in a week."

Sarah clenched her jaw. Her eyes churned with anger. Alana was suddenly terrified of her. Her acting was too good, too charged, too emotional. She was an exposed nerve.

A few people around them noticed their scene and paused to listen and watch. It wasn't clear that Alana and Sarah were "acting," and many people assumed they were having an argument about Sarah's very real baby and Alana's very real belief that she was too insane to care for her child. One older woman stared at Alana so angrily that Alana finally broke into giggles and touched Sarah's shoulder.

"I think we'd better stop. We're freaking everyone out."

Sarah giggled and wiped the real tears that had fallen from her eyes.

"But that was great," Alana told her. "You've got this. I can't imagine that anyone is better than you."

"Is it wrong that I believe that, too?"

"You're the only person who matters in this situation," Alana said. "You have to believe in yourself when nobody else does."

* * *

Sarah's audition was held the next morning at ten-thirty. Alana walked her to the theater, hugged her tightly, and watched her disappear through the dark red double-wide doors. It wasn't clear how long the audition would take, and Alana had decided to hang around the Broadway area, maybe with a cup of coffee and a book. Her stomach was flipping. She felt just as nervous as she had when she'd had to audition herself.

Alana turned to walk back into the glow of the May morning. A figure approached, but she couldn't make out any of her features because of the dark interior. And then she heard, "Alana? Alana Copperfield?"

Alana froze with surprise. She would have known that voice anywhere. "Ginny Richards?"

Ginny got close enough to show her iconic smile and big head of red curls. Alana threw her arms around her and inhaled a whiff of her perfume. It was different than the one she'd worn in their twenties. Softer and more grown-up.

"What are you doing here?" Ginny cried. "I thought you moved to Paris!"

Alana pulled back and winced. "I moved back to the States two years ago. Asher and I are divorced now."

Ginny wrinkled her nose. "Everyone I know got divorced the past few years. Seems like an epidemic."

"I usually feel sad about divorce, but not when it comes to Asher and me," Alana said. "We had a toxic relationship. And, of course, he was cheating on me. No surprise that such a prominent and successful and rich man had someone else on the side, I suppose."

"Cheating on Alana Copperfield? Who could be so stupid?" Ginny gasped.

"You're very kind," Alana said with a laugh. "I'm about to remarry, though. I'm very happy."

"And you're in New York?"

"No! I just brought my soon-to-be stepdaughter to auditions," she said. "I wanted to warn her about the theater business, but she's certain this is it for her."

"How old?"

"Nineteen. Basically, the same age I was when I came to New York to model."

"That must have been around the time we met," Ginny said, furrowing her brow.

"And now I'm almost forty-seven!" Alana said.

"I already am!"

Alana sizzled with electricity. Just looking at Ginny dropped her far, far back in her past, to a life of wild parties that went till dawn, auditions on dark theater stages and laughter that echoed through city streets that had only belonged to them. She hadn't thought of Ginny in years.

"I have to run," Ginny said, eyeing the double-wide doors. "I'm auditioning, too."

Alana raised her eyebrows with surprise. "For which role?"

"Theresa," Ginny said.

"That's a fantastic part," Alana said. "I know the play by heart by now. I've been running lines with Sarah for months."

"No chance you'd like to audition, too?" Ginny asked.

"No way. My days of acting are over."

But as she said it, Alana's heart leaped into the air and dropped back down again.

"Let's catch up tonight," Ginny said. "I have no plans. Here's my card." Ginny leafed through her purse and handed it over. "Text me. I'll take you and your daughter out!"

"Stepdaughter," Alana corrected with a big smile.

"Same difference." Ginny winked and disappeared through the door.

Alana retreated from the theater building and wandered around Broadway as her thoughts hummed with surprise. Ginny was still acting! She was still auditioning! What did that mean? Did it mean she was still fighting against women her age for a smaller number of parts? Did he mean she was short on cash and grabbing money wherever she could? Or had she actually been semi-successful in an industry that had threatened to eat so many people alive?

Alana ordered a cup of coffee and an oatmeal raisin cookie from a corner shop and watched the passers-by from the window. Being in this part of town meant spotting numerous actors and dancers or wannabe actors and dancers. They'd come from all over the world to try to make it here. "If you can make it here, you can make it anywhere," was the famous line, and it was true. But Alana hadn't made it past her glossy magazine modeling days. She hoped Sarah would make the cut.

# Chapter Three

Greta got ready for her coffee with Celeste with the nervous adrenaline she'd once associated with meeting an important editor or a famous celebrity. She tried on numerous outfits like spring dresses and slacks with nice blouses, and she redid her hair several times, pursuing a look she'd once been able to pull off. It took her more than an hour to figure out that she was attempting to look the way she had back in 2004, as though she wanted to turn back time and be the woman Celeste had known twenty years ago. But it wasn't like Greta had many photographs from that time. Her family had gone away; she hadn't bothered to record memories. Celeste was the only living memory of Greta during that time.

Bernard entered their bedroom a few minutes before she left. "You look pretty," he said as he stretched out on their bed for a nap. "Where are you going again?"

"I'm meeting a friend for coffee." Greta stretched out beside him to kiss his cheek. "Have you been writing?"

"Frantically," Bernard said. "And I think every word

of it is terrible."

Greta laughed. "I doubt that, Bernard Copperfield."

"I'm not you, darling. Not everything I write is lined with gold."

"You're the one who wrote the award-winning best-seller last year."

"I had all that time in prison to perfect it," Bernard said. "Now I'm just tired and old."

"You're not," Greta assured him. "Take a nap, and then go back upstairs and keep working."

"Aye, aye, captain." Bernard's eyelids fluttered closed.

Greta left the house a few minutes later and walked to the French café she'd adored since it opened in the early nineties. She could only count on one hand the number of times she and Celeste had gone there together. In 2003 and 2004, Greta hadn't enjoyed being seen in public. Too many Nantucketers had been angry with the Copperfields. They'd whispered about her in the corner—thinking they knew that Bernard had cheated on her with Marcia Conrad and stolen money from their dearest friends. "Don't listen to them, Greta," Celeste had urged her. "They don't know anything."

As Greta walked, she returned to that first night when Celeste had arrived in Nantucket. It had been violent outside. A storm made the Nantucket Sound froth like a big green cauldron. Greta had latched the windows and doors and hunkered in her bedroom alone with her television and her DVDs. At the time she'd been working through the entire filmography of Federico Fellini. She'd been swept up in surrealist films from the sixties and seventies. She'd been eating predominantly rice cakes slathered with bad cheese and pretending she'd never eaten anything delicious in her life.

That's when she heard a knock at the door. It was like something from a horror movie. Greta remained in her room, rigid as a stick, waiting for whoever it was to go away. But the knocks just kept coming. It sounded as though whoever it was shook the entire house—such was their desire to get in.

Finally, Greta wrapped herself in a robe and stomped downstairs. The knocks kept coming, and a flash of lightning splintered the night sky. She thought maybe a serial killer was on the other side of the door. Maybe someone had come to finish off the final Copperfield. But when she opened the door, she discovered a young woman in her early twenties. She was completely soaked to the bone, shivering. She had her fist raised as though she planned to knock all night.

"Hi! I saw your light on!" The young woman raised her chin.

Greta balked. Who was this? One of her daughters' friends, perhaps? A straggler? A hitchhiker?

And then she asked, "Is this The Copperfield House?"

Greta's knees shivered beneath her. Nobody had come looking for The Copperfield House on purpose since 1997. Six long years. She steeled herself. "It used to be The Copperfield House. But it's just an old abandoned haunted house now."

The girl started shivering. Greta's heart melted at this young woman, who was around the same age as all of her daughters, wandering through this dark and stormy night. Where were her parents?

"Do you mind if I come in for a second?" the young woman asked. "I've been traveling all day, and I'm frozen."

Greta opened the door wider and let her in. The young woman clutched her elbows and dripped across the foyer's hardwood floor. Greta hesitated. Her mothering instinct was fighting to the surface. Finally, she burst into the living room to drop logs in the fireplace, which she had up and running in just a few minutes. As the fire crackled through the tinder, she asked, "What's your name?"

"I'm Celeste. Celeste Harding." Her voice wavered.

"Why don't you go to the second floor to take a hot shower, Celeste?" Greta turned to look the young woman in the eye. "Use the clean towel beneath the sink. I'll have some hot food ready for you down here when you get out."

Celeste's lips parted with surprise. Perhaps she hadn't anticipated such kindness from a stranger. Greta hadn't anticipated giving it. But as she went up and the staircase creaked, Greta was transported back to a time when owning and operating The Copperfield House had meant being a caretaker for all sorts of people. Her heart ached at the memory.

And suddenly, she'd been struck with the thought, *I won't be able to take it when she goes away.*

* * *

Greta reached the French café a few minutes before the time she and Celeste had agreed upon. She sat in a shard of sunlight toward the back of the large room with its wooden walls and square wooden tables that featured wooden vases filled with lilies. She ordered a cappuccino and sat nervously until she heard footsteps to her left. She was on her feet. But when she turned, she found a meek-looking woman with ratty hair and a bad hot pink sweater approaching her. She didn't look anything like Celeste. Greta sighed and sat back down. But the woman continued to approach her. Was she planning on sitting at the table beside her? The room was empty save for Greta. It didn't make sense. But now, the woman stood over her table, smiling at her. Greta flinched and forced her eyes to hers. It couldn't be. Could it?

"Greta," the woman said.

Greta was on her feet. She peered into this woman's eyes, searching for her darling Celeste. But this woman looked so tired and withdrawn. Her cheeks were hollow, her skin was ghoulish, and her clothing decisions were atrocious. Greta opened her arms and said, "Celeste! It's you!" She hugged her with her eyes open as her head throbbed with surprise. Even in her arms, Celeste didn't feel the same. It was a strange contrast to seeing Julia, Alana, and Ella again. They'd been almost identical to their teenage selves. She'd known them to their core.

Celeste ordered a decaf coffee and sat next to Greta with a smile that showed how yellow her teeth had gotten. Greta's heart flipped over.

"You look wonderful," Celeste told her. "Just the same as ever."

Greta wasn't sure what to say. "You look great. I couldn't believe it when I heard from you. It had been so long."

Celeste furrowed her brow. "Too long. You're right."

There was a strange pause. Greta couldn't remember any pauses between her and Celeste during the year and four months they'd spent together twenty years ago. Their conversations had burned with fire, light and creativity.

"What brings you to Nantucket?" Greta asked.

"A short vacation," Celeste explained. "My husband and I are here for some sailing and sightseeing."

*Just like everyone else,* Greta thought.

"Your husband?"

"Brad," Celeste said. "He's an accountant."

Greta's heart seized. How could Celeste have married an accountant who took normal vacations? Provocative and artistic and wild Celeste? Celeste, who'd arrived in the midst of a storm that had turned the Nantucket Sound green?

But Greta was polite. She had to be. She asked questions about Brad, which inevitably led to a conversation about their children.

"I have four," Celeste said. "Didn't you have four?"

"Yes." Greta was having trouble keeping her smile up. This was such a boring, everyday conversation. She could have had it with the woman at the grocery store. "They all came back to Nantucket two years ago. It's been a thrill to get to know my grandchildren. The Copperfield House is all filled up again. We even restarted the residency."

Celeste sipped her coffee. "And how has that been?"

"Great. We've had a few dramas here and there. My granddaughter Anna fell in love with one of our writers recently. That was chaotic. She'd just had a baby."

Celeste kept smiling, an easy smile that Greta found difficult to read. Greta had to stop herself from bursting with the question she burned with about what Celeste had done professionally. What had happened after she'd gone to New York City in 2004? But Celeste seemed unwilling to talk about that. She spoke at length about her children, about her eldest son's belief in good attendance, about her youngest son's desire to be an accountant like his father. She spoke about the birds in their garden and about a trip they'd taken to Florida last year. The conversation was easy and uncomplicated. It provided the dullest of information.

"You should have seen my husband and me last summer when we decided to get the garden going again," Celeste was saying. "We argued for hours at a time about what kind of tomatoes to put in!" She laughed easily.

Greta tried to join her. But her heart felt cracked around the edges. They'd been at the coffee shop for more than an hour, and Celeste hadn't brought up her writing career once. Greta had always assumed she was her number-one protégée, that her skills rivaled even Greta's, and that Celeste would have the career that Greta had always longed for.

When Celeste finished her coffee, she admitted she had to meet her husband at their hotel shortly. "But it's been lovely to see you," she said.

Greta wanted to demand answers. Why had Celeste wanted to see Greta if all she planned to talk about was her daughter's favorite type of sandwich? Why hadn't they gotten down to the root of their relationship? Why hadn't they mentioned anything about their time together? And already she planned to go!

"Okay," Greta said. "It's been good to see you, too."

Greta stood to hug Celeste. The hug was slightly longer than she would have liked; it seemed to represent a different kind of relationship. Celeste turned and whisked out of the French coffee shop and back out of Greta's life. Greta had a hunch that she would never see her again, and she was usually correct about these sorts of things. She had whiplash. She sat back down and ordered a cup of tea.

# Chapter Four

Ginny had always known the best places. Bars, restaurants, exclusive clubs, she'd always found her way onto guest lists and into exclusive parties as though she had the right of way through life. It had mystified Alana back in the early days of their time in the city together, although it hadn't taken Alana long to figure out Ginny's secrets. Alana had soon known all the right people, too, until she'd left all that behind.

Alana felt swept back into Ginny's world. It was hard to believe she'd ever left.

But this time, she had Sarah in tow. Sarah was a brilliant actress, but she couldn't even keep her excitement at bay. "I heard about this restaurant on TikTok!" she whispered as she followed Alana and Ginny up the stairs into a Chinese place celebrities frequented. "The waitlist is crazy long!"

Sarah's guess was as good as Alana's as to how Ginny had gotten them in. Eventually, she struck up the nerve to ask, and Ginny shrugged and said, "I used to date the guy who owned it." She left it at that. Sarah's eyes widened.

Ginny led them to a corner table with a view of the restaurant. Everything shone neon, and waiters and waitresses were dressed beautifully and exotically as though they'd just stepped out of the ancient Chinese past. They brought fancy wet napkins for them to wash their hands with, then served them sparkling water and champagne. Although Alana knew all about teenage drinking (she'd been a big fan of it back in the day), Alana never let Sarah drink in front of her. She could do that on her own time and away from her father's prying eyes. Alana wanted no part of it. But the champagne was exquisite. When Ginny suggested they give Sarah a small sip, Sarah looked at Alana pleadingly as Alana winced and said, "Your dad would kill me."

"It's the right thing," Ginny said. "You'll be twenty-one in no time."

Sarah looked disgruntled as she pored over the menu, but the dark cloud soon dissipated, and the three of them had a marvelous time. Both Ginny and Sarah were confident about their auditions, although Sarah admitted her tone of voice had been "weird" halfway through. "It was like I was self-sabotaging," she said. "I totally panicked."

"I'm sure it was great," Alana said.

"I've worked with the director before," Ginny said. "He's a great guy. Very charming. Very insightful. He told me I'm basically a shoo-in for the part." She blushed and sipped her champagne. "But I like auditioning anyway. It forces me to get in tune with the character early on."

"How many times have you worked with this director?" Alana asked.

"Five or six times," Ginny said.

Alana's heart thumped. "You've had quite the career, then?"

"I had to figure something out. I didn't want to leave New York, and I didn't want to quit acting. I've worked off-Broadway and even several student films to get by. There were a few years here and there where I had to work behind the bar or as a waitress, but I always ended up back on stage." Ginny flipped her hair. "I'm addicted! I hope I get to act as a little old lady one day."

Sarah gushed. "That's amazing. If I don't get into the play, I would love to sit in on rehearsals sometimes and watch you work."

"I don't see why not," Ginny said. "But don't count yourself out yet, honey. Anything can happen. Maybe the gods of theater will shine down upon you."

Sarah chuckled and glanced at Alana. Alana sensed herself dimming in Sarah's eyes. Ginny had had a marvelous and long-drawn-out career. No, she'd never been a superstar as Alana had been for the briefest of moments. But she'd kept it going, kept getting roles. And now she was supposedly the number-one pick for the director. That meant something.

Suddenly, Ginny's phone buzzed. She grabbed it and answered frantically, "Hello?"

Sarah and Alana watched her expectantly. Alana's heart was in her throat.

"Thank you so much," Ginny said as tears filled her eyes. "I can't wait to work with you again, too." She hung up and brought both fists into the air in triumph. It was obvious she'd gotten the part.

"It's for sure?" Sarah asked with surprise.

"Yes. I'm in," Ginny said.

Sarah bowed her head and looked at her phone. "Nobody has called me yet."

"It's important to enjoy yourself tonight, no matter

what," Ginny said. She sounded frantic and slightly unhinged. It was clear she was already envisioning the next weeks of her life, the new play, a new group of cast members, and new rehearsals. Alana remembered that period of a new production well when everything shifted on its axis, and it was as though everything was possible because nothing had happened yet.

Suddenly, Sarah's phone began to ring. It was a surprising sound, louder than Alana remembered. Alana learned later it was the first time Sarah had turned it all the way up. Sarah pounced on it. "Hello?" Sarah was breathless. Alana watched as her face transformed like an opening flower. And then she was on her feet saying, "Thank you! Thank you! I can't wait! Thank you!"

Ginny and Alana burst up to wrap Sarah in hugs. Alana couldn't believe it. The doors of Broadway that had once closed for Alana had been flung open for Sarah. They were welcoming her into the fold.

"I'm so thrilled!" Ginny cried. "We're going to be stage buddies!"

Alana panged with many feelings. She never would have admitted to anyone that she was jealous. That her stomach felt twisted with it. Ginny's life was looking better and brighter by the minute—especially as Alana sipped more and more champagne. Had she given up on her dreams too early? Had she thrown her life in the trash?

But to ask that question meant poring over the details of her almost forty-seven years. It meant asking if her first marriage had been a mistake from the start. It meant asking if she never should have been a model and rather focused on acting the entire time. Ginny had never been a supermodel; her face had never been on the cover of

Vogue or flashing up in Times Square. But she still surged forward. Did that mean she'd won?

Alana refused to allow her strange regrets to destroy the night. They ate at the Chinese restaurant and immediately went dancing at a club that allowed eighteen and up. Sarah shimmied across the dance floor and glowed with adrenaline. Ginny whispered in Alana's ear and asked, "Doesn't she remind you of us at that age? Isn't it crazy?" Alana laughed and said, "She's a whole lot smarter than I was at that age. That's for sure." Ginny agreed and joined Sarah on the dance floor. She had more energy than Alana did.

They stopped dancing sometime around one in the morning. They paraded down the street and grabbed slices of pizza at a late-night pizzeria, where they laughed about nothing in particular. They acted as raucous as three teenagers.

"I have a feeling Sarah's going to get me in trouble this summer!" Ginny cried as she tapped parmesan onto her pizza.

"Me? I'm not the troublemaker. You were the one flirting with those guys earlier," Sarah teased.

It was true that Ginny seemed keen to flirt with every man who walked by. She was gorgeous and vivacious and clever, and they always went along with it. Alana wasn't jealous of that. She didn't want to be single, and she loved Jeremy deep in her bones.

But sometimes, she caught herself stirring in jealousy about Ginny's freedom and career and openness to the wildness of life. Was Alana boring by comparison? Did Sarah think she was boring because she'd given up and started a school for acting rather than pursuing her own art?

She thought of Ella's tour, Julia's publishing house, her mother and father's books and Quentin's documentaries. Compared to them, Alana was an artistic failure. No wonder her mother liked her least. Of all the Copperfields, she'd been the first to give up on her art. What did that say about her?

Of course, it was just a guess that Greta liked Alana least of all. But it was something Alana had never been able to shake. Sometimes, she wondered if that was the reason she hadn't had children. She knew that a mother's love wasn't always a given. She didn't want to disappoint them. And she didn't want them not to love her back.

It was protection. But it still hadn't protected Alana from the sorrows that lurked in the shadows of life.

* * *

Alana and Sarah set aside the next morning to search for a temporary apartment for Sarah's summer in the city. Their budget was tight because Sarah didn't want to ask her father for any cash; she wanted to support herself completely. This was admirable and rare in this generation, Alana knew. But she considered telling Sarah to push aside her pride; some of the places they looked online at were dingy and dangerous, and Jeremy would pull out all the stops for his little girl. But eventually they discovered a tiny studio apartment in the Lower East Side that fit Sarah's price range. Sarah called the landlord (she wanted to do that herself, too) and set up an appointment to see the place that afternoon. Until then, they had time to kill.

"We should go wedding dress shopping!" Sarah suggested. "Unless you want to wait for your sisters."

Alana blushed and sipped her coffee. She'd imagined herself trying on dresses surrounded by Julia, Ella, and her mother. But something about Sarah's smile made her leap at the chance. She'd chosen this life with Sarah and Jeremy. She hadn't chosen the life of off-Broadway or off-off-Broadway. She needed to celebrate that choice with the perfect dress. It didn't hurt to look.

Sarah jumped in the shower before they left, which gave Alana time to call Jeremy. He already knew Sarah's good news, but he sounded wary. "I'm so glad you're going with her to look at this apartment," he said. "If the landlord is shady in any way, don't let her sign."

"Don't worry. I know my way around shady landlords," Alana assured him.

"I don't know what to feel about any of this," Jeremy said.

Alana could picture him in the basement of the Nantucket Records' Office beneath his fluorescent lamp. Sometimes, he wore reading glasses that he played with when he was nervous.

"Sarah's a smart girl," Alana said. "And a brilliant actress. She deserves to give this a chance. And we're going to help her every step of the way."

"Not really," Jeremy said. "She refuses my help money-wise." He sounded fearful about that, too. As though money was the final link between himself and Sarah, and he didn't want to give it up.

"She loves you, Jeremy," Alana assured him. "The help and guidance you give from here on out has nothing to do with money. We should celebrate that."

Alana and Sarah left the hotel and headed toward the first of Sarah's selected wedding dress shops. "I heard about this place on TikTok," Sarah explained as they walked by the window and gazed inside. "A YouTube star I like went here for her wedding dress."

Alana's throat filled with dread. She had a hunch that was soon confirmed when they walked in and realized that none of the wedding dresses had price tags. What did that mean for the prices? Sarah suggested they play it cool and pick out a few dresses for Alana to try on. It was true that the gowns were stunning, made in glowing fabrics that seemed to have been spun in heaven. The sales clerk helped Alana and hung three dresses in a dressing room bigger than the foyer in The Copperfield House. Sarah helped Alana into the first gown and then stepped back so that Alana could swirl around and look at her reflection in all six of the mirrors. Alana pulled her shoulders back and imagined herself on her wedding day in this gown.

"It's a little much, isn't it?" Alana said with a laugh. "I'm not Carrie Bradshaw. I'm not marrying Mr. Big."

Sarah had just watched *Sex and the City* for the first time and cackled happily. "You're right. Dad would probably run the other way if you wore this down the aisle. He doesn't do well with ostentatious."

Alana wrinkled her nose at the other dresses they'd picked out. They were all similarly heavy and wildly over-the-top. Before she chickened out, she pressed open the dressing room door and called to the clerk, "Ma'am? How much does this dress cost?" She referred to the dress she was wearing.

The clerk looked at her as though she had three heads. People weren't supposed to ask questions like that. It was gauche.

Under her breath, the clerk answered, "Thirty-five thousand dollars."

Although she was fully freaking out, Alana made sure

not to change her facial expression. "Thank you." She closed the door and locked eyes with Sarah, who giggled into her hand.

"Let's get out of here," Alana said.

Alana had never removed a garment with more fear. She stepped out of the dress and hung it gingerly on the hook, then hurriedly put on her street clothes and ran out of there. She and Sarah hit the sidewalk and burst into giggles. By the time they'd rounded the corner, Alana had tears in her eyes.

"That was insane, Sarah!" Alana cried.

"I know. I'm sorry. I didn't even know they made dresses that cost that much."

"That woman almost killed me," Alana said. "But I had to know."

They carried on through Midtown and went in and out of wedding dress shops all through the afternoon. Alana had given up finding "the one" that day when they stumbled into the boutique near Sarah's would-be apartment. They planned to just dip in and out so they wouldn't be late for Sarah's appointment with the landlord. But the dress that hung in the corner gave Alana pause. It was vintage-looking with a Parisian air, similar to a dress a French friend of Alana's had worn a few years back during her wedding at Versailles. Alana's fingers buzzed with excitement. Sarah caught Alana's expression. "Try it on."

"We don't have time," Alana said.

"We have enough time."

Alana rolled her eyes and ducked into the dressing room. Because it wasn't as ornate or heavy as the other one, she got herself into the dress in no time flat. When she whipped open the door, Sarah's face told her everything she needed to know: that she looked like a bride.

Alana took one look at herself in the mirror and knew in the belly of her soul that this was the one. But she didn't have time to linger on this decision. They had to hurry to Sarah's apartment. They couldn't delay.

Alana asked the clerk to hold the dress as they went around the corner to meet the landlord. He was a drab-looking Englishman named Edmund, whose father had bought the apartment as an investment. "Nobody could have imagined how expensive this place would get!" he said with a laugh.

Alana watched Sarah move through the apartment with the air of a young woman about to build the life of her dreams. She asked questions about utilities and where to put the garbage and then agreed to sign for the summer —with the possibility of extending the contract. The apartment was furnished, which made it easier for everyone for the time being. Alana co-signed the contract and shook Edmund's hand. They would move Sarah in on June 1st. That was two days before rehearsals began.

Alana and Sarah returned to the hotel that night to freshen up and prepare for their final evening before returning home. Sarah was bubbly and smiling at everyone. They should bottle that feeling, Alana thought. The feeling that everything was about to begin. The feeling that nothing could ever go wrong. It would sell for millions of dollars. It was the secret to youth.

# Chapter Five

It was Greta's idea to invite the girls over to celebrate Sarah's new off-Broadway play. Alana, Ella, Julia, and Sarah had agreed to join her on the back patio that evening for barbecue chicken and margaritas. But it was still hours before they'd show up. This left Greta alone in the kitchen, stirring up a homemade barbecue sauce and thinking about the past. Ever since she'd met Celeste the other day, she'd felt haunted.

Greta remembered the first week of Celeste's stay at The Copperfield House back in 2003. Greta had put Celeste in Julia's old bedroom rather than putting her up in the residency half of the house so that she didn't have to heat that half of the house on colder nights. It was a strange June; the weather turned on a dime. Celeste was very quiet those first few days. When Greta asked her how she'd heard about The Copperfield House, Celeste said only that her brother had once lived at the residency. He was a writer like she was. Greta couldn't help but take the bait. One night, over dinner of roasted potatoes and salmon, Greta asked, "So. You're a writer. That's why you wanted to come here. I'd love to see what you're working on."

It had been a long time since Greta had cared about anyone's art. Most of all, her own.

Celeste showed her poetry collection sheepishly. Greta took the poems and prepared herself to be disappointed. She prepared herself to say, "They're pretty good, but they need work. Here and here and here." But instead, the poetry blew her socks off. She sat up all night by the fire and read through the poems as tears dried on her cheeks. This young woman had captured something about loneliness and heartache that Greta, in her fifties, had never managed with her own writing. Celeste was like Sylvia Plath reincarnated. She had a captivating power.

Greta kept her tone even when she told Celeste that she knew a publisher in New York City who might be interested in publishing Celeste's poetry chapbook. Celeste brightened with surprise. They were in the kitchen over bowls of oatmeal, sipping coffee. Greta had a strange thought, *"If I can get this girl's chapbook published, I'll feel useful again. I'll feel a part of the world."*

Over the next four weeks, Greta helped Celeste reorder the poems so that the chapbook was seamless and powerful. They sent the poems to the publisher and celebrated with wine on the back porch. Celeste still hadn't told Greta where she'd come from or why, but Greta decided she didn't care. They laughed together. They exchanged poems they loved by long-dead poets who'd captivated their hearts. And Greta felt her own heart opening up bit by bit after six years of darkness.

But now—so many years after 2003—Celeste was a

shell of a woman. Greta could not let it go. What had happened to her? Why had it happened between those magical nights in 2003 and now that had allowed Celeste to crumble?

Julia arrived fifteen minutes before she said she would. She'd brought ingredients for tequila and sat cross-legged at the kitchen table, mixing a big pitcher for everyone and chatting about a few books she planned to publish with her publishing house that summer. She had a brilliant mind and a creative intellect that sometimes floored Greta and Bernard. She was every bit their daughter, though—in ways Alana wasn't.

Ella wasn't biologically their daughter in the first place. But Greta never dwelled on that fact.

"And how are Anna and Adam? I keep missing them," Greta asked about her granddaughter and newest great-grandson as she slid the barbecue chicken into the oven.

"Brilliant as ever. Anna and Smith are smitten," Julia said dreamily, speaking of the newest writer produced by The Copperfield House who'd fallen in love with Anna. "Charlie and I had them over for dinner the other night, and Smith held the baby for hours to give Anna a break. I like to think she's found someone who will protect her and Adam like that. Who will think of their needs above his own."

It had been a fear of Greta's after Anna's fiancé's death: who would care for her and the baby? Who would ever want to marry someone who'd gone through so much at such a young age? But Smith had been through his own trials. He was a writer. He didn't shy away from the messiness of life.

Alana, Sarah, and Ella arrived with another Copperfield in tow—Laura, Ella's daughter, who was in from the city. Laura had just finished her second year at Columbia and was staying in the city that summer for an internship. As they paraded through the house, she gushed to Sarah about what a fantastic time they would have together. Greta beamed and welcomed her daughters, granddaughter, and soon-to-be step-granddaughter into her arms.

"Congratulations, Sarah!" she cried. "I hear you're a force to be reckoned with."

Sarah laughed nervously. "I don't know about that. I couldn't believe it when he called to say I'd gotten the part. I'd basically talked myself out of it."

"You should never talk yourself out of something you want in your bones," Greta warned. "Nobody else in that city believes in you. You have to do all the believing yourself."

Sarah's smile widened. She seemed to be an intelligent and optimistic young woman with enough talent to go the distance in that cut-throat environment. Greta eyed Alana and hunted for clues of jealousy. Greta would have empathized. During her twenty-five years of anonymity and hiding out at The Copperfield House, she'd felt the rest of the world go on without her. She'd felt she'd given up.

But she was back to writing like crazy. It was proof that there were numerous phases in life. You just had to be strong enough to live through them.

Over dinner, Sarah talked at length about her apartment and the play. Greta asked numerous questions about how Sarah got into character, the backstory of the playwright and the resumé of the director until Alana came right out and asked if Greta wanted to come to New York City to help Sarah move in on June 1st. Greta was taken aback and laughed.

"Is it that obvious that I'm so intrigued?" Greta asked.

"It's not a long trip," Alana assured her.

"I'm not as strong as I once was. I don't know how I can help you move furniture or boxes or anything like that."

"'I'm only bringing the basics," Sarah said. "The apartment is furnished, and I'll be at rehearsals all summer anyway."

Greta swelled with excitement. She imagined herself in the Lower East Side, surrounded by the bustling city, chatting to neighbors on the front stoops, grabbing a bagel for breakfast. She imagined herself to be fifty years younger and living an alternate version of her life. It was a shame you didn't get to do it many different times in many different places.

"I'll go," Greta said. "Just tell me how I can help."

It was settled.

That evening, after the girls went off in their separate directions, Greta sat on the back porch alone with a cup of tea. Bernard surprised her with a knock on the door.

"Can I join you? Or do you want to be alone?"

"Please," Greta said. "You know I love your company."

Bernard sat beside her with a cup of tea and folded his hands on the tabletop. The sun plotted its final course into the ocean and cast everything in an orange sheen.

"Alana tells me you're off to New York City."

Greta laughed. "It's silly, isn't it? I just want to experience a little bit of Sarah's off-Broadway magic."

"I think it means a lot to Alana that you want to join."

Greta arched her brow and watched as a seagull swept lazily through the sky. "Maybe." She could feel Bernard watching her curiously.

"Can I ask you something?"

"Sure," Greta said.

"You've been quiet ever since you got back from the coffee shop the other day. Did something happen?"

Greta turned to look at him. She should have known he would notice a shift in her behavior. This was Bernard Copperfield, the novelist and king of nuance. She couldn't get anything past him.

"It's hard to explain," Greta said.

"Try me."

Greta took a sip of tea and swept through her memories. It was difficult to know how to explain something so tender. "I met with a friend I hadn't seen in twenty years. She was a young poet and playwright. She stayed at The Copperfield House between 2003 and 2004, and we became very good friends. I thought she would become someone incredible. Someone the world would know. But she faded into obscurity. And when I saw her the other day, I hardly recognized her. I feel that something happened to her. Something that made her hide from the world. But I don't know what."

Bernard furrowed his brow. "Wow."

Greta laughed. "Too much?"

"No. I should have known it was a doozy." Bernard thought for a moment. "You can tell me if this is off the mark. But it seems to me that Celeste helped you through a difficult time. You think she's in a difficult time now, and you want to help her through that, too."

Greta perked up. "I think you hit the nail on the head."

Could it really be that simple? Could Greta approach Celeste and ask her what was wrong and how she could help? Celeste had said she lived in New Jersey with her husband and children. She had her number. She could text Celeste and meet up with her when she went to the city with Alana and Sarah. Her heart thrummed with excitement. *I should have said something immediately. That was probably why Celeste reached out to me in the first place. She needs help. She needs the sort of guidance she's come to expect from Greta Copperfield.*

"Bernard, you're a genius," Greta said before throwing her arms around him.

That night, Greta texted Celeste:

> "Wonderful to see you the other day. I'm coming to the city on June 1st, and I would love to come to New Jersey to see where you live and meet your family. What do you say?"

Greta felt the text to be magnanimous and kind. She felt sure Celeste would text within the hour to make a date. But that night, she received no word from Celeste. She received nothing the next day, either. When she mentioned this to Bernard, he said, *"She has kids. I'm sure she's just busy."* But by the end of the week, Celeste hadn't answered, and Greta was worried. Maybe Celeste hadn't been impressed with Greta during their meeting. Maybe she'd thought less of her. Worse, maybe Celeste was embarrassed about her state and career and had decided to hide herself.

Greta sent seven text messages over the next couple of weeks, but none of them were answered. She decided to put this quest to bed. It was clear Celeste didn't want anything to do with her anyway.

# Chapter Six

Jeremy packed up the truck with Sarah's bags long before they needed to depart. With so much time to spare and nothing to do, he became jittery and agitated, asking Sarah numerous questions that had no bearing on today's move. "Did your landlord tell you if he's charging for extra air conditioning? It'll get hot this summer." "What about cell phone data? Is the signal strong up there?" "You remember that you have to get a good eight hours of sleep every night? I don't want that rash to creep back up again." Sarah rubbed her temples. He was just stressing her out even more. Alana eventually stuck up for Sarah and said, "Everything is under control, J! Sarah's got this. We're just helping her move her stuff from point A to point B." Jeremy rubbed the back of his neck sheepishly and tried to pour himself another cup of coffee, but Alana cut him off. "We don't need you any more nervous than you already are."

But soon, it was officially time to go. Jeremy drove Sarah and Alana to The Copperfield House to pick up

Alana's mother. Greta had packed an overnight bag for their stay at the same hotel Alana and Sarah had opted for a couple of weeks ago. She looked vibrant and excited. She leaped into the backseat with more energy than most teenagers and burst into a dialogue with Sarah about her character's motivations. Apparently, Greta had spent all night reading the play and had memorized some of the lines. Just like Alana, she was soaking up Sarah's success. But it was adorable to see.

Alana felt this was the Copperfield way of officially bringing Sarah into the family. They adored her. She fit the mold.

On the ferry, Alana and Jeremy cozied up along the railing, and Greta and Sarah grabbed coffees at the kiosk inside. Jeremy muttered in Alana's ear, "Why couldn't she fall in love with something that she could do closer to home? Teaching? Heck, she could work with me at the Nantucket Records Office!"

"She doesn't want to work with her father in a base-ment," Alana said with a laugh. She kissed him. "She loves her father to pieces. But she has to go after her dreams."

Alana's stomach tightened as a little voice in the back of her head said, *you gave up on your dreams, remember? You're nothing.* That voice had been consistent ever since their trip to New York City. And she hated it! No matter how often she told the voice how happy she was and how excited she was about her upcoming wedding, the voice of discontent grew louder and louder. She remembered how her mother used to tell her, *"You're the kind of teenage girl who can never be happy."* She wondered if she was also the kind of woman who could never be happy. Not really.

And Jeremy didn't deserve that! He deserved a woman with no doubts at all.

They reached the Lower East Side by lunchtime. Sarah popped out of the truck to get the keys from the landlord as Jeremy spent the next thirty minutes looking for a decent parking spot. "This is why you shouldn't move to the city!" he grumbled. Alana reminded him, "That's why people don't have cars in the city."

Sarah came back to grab a few bags and led them into the apartment. Alana watched Jeremy as he inspected every nick and cranny of the little place, opened the cupboards, looked under the bed, and checked to make sure the toilet was flushed. He was frantic as any good father should be. Alana's mother sat at the edge of the bed, smiling to herself.

"What are you thinking about?" Alana asked.

"I'm thinking about my little apartment in Paris," Greta said. "It was so tiny! But it was all mine, and I loved it. As far as I was concerned, it was all I needed in the world." She sniffed. "It's funny that your father and I went on to buy that enormous house. It must be a thousand times bigger than my old apartment."

"And a thousand times bigger than this one," Sarah chimed in. "But it's home."

"That's right!" Greta smiled.

They spent the afternoon doing everything they could to ensure Sarah's first week would run smoothly. They purchased toiletries and groceries from a local store; they got her fancy espresso for a little French press she'd gotten for Christmas; they took a walk with her around the neighborhood so she could get their bearings. Jeremy started to get excited at some point, talking about the historic architecture and the beautiful parks filled with old trees. Alana strung her arm through his and listened to the rhythm of their conversation. These were three people she loved so much it hurt. She realized that Greta would have loved to be there to move her to New York City back when she'd done it. But she'd gone with Asher instead. She'd latched herself to a man in a way Greta hadn't understood or respected.

It was hard not to hold herself accountable for that.

Ginny invited them to a beautiful Italian restaurant that evening in Little Italy. Alana explained to her mother how she knew Ginny, giving a brief overview of their tremendously electrifying years together in New York City.

Greta said, "And she's still working as an actress? How wonderful!"

And again, Alana sizzled with jealousy. Would her mother respect her more if she was doing that?

Ginny was a few minutes late. Alana, Jeremy, Greta, and Sarah waited nervously in the foyer of the restaurant, stealing glances at the gorgeous diners peppered across the room. Their faces were illuminated with candles. Ginny entered with the flourish of a performer and threw her arms around Alana.

"And you must be the famous Greta Copperfield!" Ginny said. "Alana always gushed about your work."

Greta looked momentarily confused. "Alana gushed about my work. I don't buy it."

But it was true, Alana remembered. She'd been obsessed with her mother's brilliance and Alana's apparent lack of brilliance. Despite having her face in Times Square, she'd felt like a failure in her mother's eyes. And she'd always talked about it when it got too late into the night or the morning. Ginny and those in her close circle knew Alana's pain and torment. She wasn't sure she'd ever shared it fully with Asher, though. Perhaps that was proof of something.

They were seated. Ginny ordered olives and tiny sausages, as well as Aperol spritzes with orange slices. When they didn't card Sarah, Jeremy decided to look the other way. Sarah looked gleeful and promised, "Just one, Dad." Jeremy shrugged and said, "You're on your own now. I know you'll take care of yourself." He gave her a look of tenderness mixed with fear.

"I'll take care of her," Ginny promised. "We're in almost every scene together, aren't we, doll?" She laughed. "I'll make sure she shows up every day to rehearsal."

"I appreciate that," Jeremy answered seriously.

Greta sipped her Aperol spritz and looked at Ginny. "You have to tell me about your career," she said. "You've been at this a long time."

Alana's stomach twisted.

"Maybe too long!" Ginny laughed. "But it's true. I came to the city a few months before my nineteenth birthday, and I never left. I've worked with just about every theater company in the city. Many of them have closed up shop over the years. It's a tragedy. New York is a city that pours money into the arts, but times have changed everywhere, even here."

Alana's mother's eyes glinted with intrigue. "Out of curiosity, did you ever work with the Winsome Theater Company?"

Ginny's smile fell, and she tilted her head. "Goodness, yes. Years and years ago. They closed up in 2008 or 2009, right?"

Greta raised one of her shoulders. "What years were you with them?"

"Must have been 2006 till they disbanded," Ginny answered. "Are you familiar with their productions?"

"Maybe," Greta said. Her voice was very soft and uneven.

*What was going on?* Alana felt the air shift and tighten over the table. Greta was looking at Ginny as though she were a ghost.

"Do you happen to know someone named Celeste Harding?" Greta asked.

Ginny's eyes filled with tears. Alana was so startled that she set down her olive.

"You know her." Greta sounded excited. "Did you perform her plays?"

Ginny reached for a napkin and pressed it over her eyes. Alana burned with curiosity. She locked eyes with Jeremy over the table and raised her shoulders. Greta's face fell.

"I didn't mean to upset you," Greta said. "She's an old friend of mine."

Ginny allowed the napkin to fall from her face. She gaped at Greta for a long time. And then she said, "You don't know, do you?"

"What don't I know?" Greta asked, straightening her posture as though she were preparing to take an enormous blow.

"We just lost her last week," Ginny said. "Breast cancer. It happened so quickly. I didn't even hear about it until after the funeral."

Alana turned to watch her mother melt on the spot. Ginny was wordless. Greta burst up and muttered, "I'm sorry. I just need a minute," before running toward the bathroom and disappearing. Alana hesitated and then stood to follow after her. *Celeste Harding?* Alana had never heard that name before, but that didn't mean anything. People were always coming in and out of The Copperfield House. The timing was strange, though. Ginny had known Celeste from 2006 to 2009—years when Greta had apparently been locked up inside The Copperfield House and refusing to see anyone. The Copperfield House closed its doors in 1997. Had she known her before that?

Alana entered the bathroom and knocked on the stall that held her mother. She was sniffling. "Mom? Are you all right?"

The bathroom door opened just a crack to show Greta's face. It was hard and stoic, as though she wanted to hide her tears from her eldest.

"I'm sorry for your loss, Mom," Alana said because she didn't know what else to say.

Greta's chin quivered. "If it's all the same to you, I'd like to go home now."

Alana was suddenly terrified. Greta wasn't the sort of woman to run home to cry.

"We can't go home right now. The Hyannis ferries don't run all night." Alana felt strange delivering this news to her mother, who probably knew the ferry schedules like the back of her hand. "But you can go to our hotel early if you like. I booked you a separate room." Alana wet her lips as her mother continued to stare right through her. "I could take you there now if you like."

Greta crossed her arms tightly over her chest like a child might.

"Who is Celeste Harding?" Alana finally asked.

"I'd like to go back to the hotel," Greta said firmly. "But I can go by myself. Don't worry about me."

She stalked past Alana in a role reversal fit for an Oscar and retreated into the dining room. Alana followed after her and watched as she grabbed her bag, nodded to the others, and stepped into the night. She was gone.

# Chapter Seven

Greta hurried into the streets of Little Italy with her heart in her throat. Alana had sent a link of the hotel name and address, and she waved her arm to try to grab a taxi before giving up and walking all the way there. She shimmied through crowds of New Yorkers and tourists, hurried along grimy sidewalks and paused at crosswalks as her thoughts swirled and threatened to bring her to tears. She couldn't believe this. Celeste Harding was dead.

Greta reached the front desk of the hotel and checked in with a young woman who sensed Greta was upset. She fetched her a glass of water and said she was sending a glass of champagne to her room "on the house." Greta could barely see her; her tears had begun to fall. When she reached the room upstairs, she collapsed on the bed and stared at a crack that wound its way across the ceiling. On her phone were twelve missed calls from Alana, and she texted:

"I'm fine. I just need to rest."

How could she explain herself?

Greta had packed her lightweight laptop just in case the mood struck her to write. Her agent was after her for a new book because the Copperfield name was especially famous right now; she wanted to ride that wave. Greta propped herself up on pillows and googled Celeste Harding for the second time in two weeks. This time, an obituary popped up.

The photograph they'd used was taken from Celeste's years at the Winsome Theater Company. She glowed with a smile that spoke of many years of future prosperity and tremendous intellect. This was the young woman Greta had known and loved. But the obituary was brief and mysterious. "Celeste Harding Green passed away on May 23, 2024, after a brief illness. She is survived by those who loved her the most: her husband, Dan, and her four children, Vincent, Bailey, Lyla, and Kyle." It offered no information. It filled in no gaps.

Greta closed her computer and got under the covers. She brought herself back to that day at the French café with Celeste on May 14th. She remembered how judgmental she'd been, how she'd looked at Celeste's clothes and sniffed with confusion. She remembered wondering why on earth Celeste had reached out to Greta if all she wanted to talk about was her son Vincent's perfect school attendance and her recent trip to Florida.

Why hadn't Celeste told her what was happening?

Greta felt as though she floated through the ocean without a life raft. She felt frustrated at times and terribly sad at other times.

She wondered why a woman on the brink of death wouldn't have wanted to say exactly what was on her mind. Celeste had had nothing to lose. But she'd spoken about mundane things, then gone to meet her husband, the accountant, for dinner. Now, she was dead. It didn't add up.

Greta had gone into "hiding" in 1997, but she hadn't really been in hiding because everyone had known where she was. She was at The Copperfield House. She'd locked her doors and locked her heart. The reasons had been clear. Bernard was in prison. Her children hated their family. The daydream of her life was over.

Something had happened to Celeste, too. Something before the cancer. Something that had blotted out her light. Did anyone know what that was?

Before Greta knew what she was doing, she had her agent on the phone. Cynthia was a woman in her early forties who regularly sold books for six figures but hadn't allowed her success to go to her head. Greta liked her because she could run ideas past her without judgment. Cynthia was very clear if something was a bad idea or not. She knew what she could sell.

"Greta! This is a surprise," Cynthia said.

"I wanted to call you right away," Greta said, "because I have an idea for a novel. And I don't want to follow it too far down the rabbit hole if it's a bad one."

"What a pleasure. Shoot."

Celeste's face floated in Greta's mind's eye as she said, "I want to write a mystery about loss of ambition. I want to write a story of an American woman with talent and brains, a young woman set to go the distance who ultimately fails because of the extenuating circumstances of her life. It's really a story about everyone in America. About how difficult it is to overcome your past and your family and your decisions."

Greta could feel Cynthia's smile over the phone.

"That sounds like a huge undertaking," Cynthia said. "And incredibly vague."

"I know. I know. I have a lot to flesh out," Greta said as a blush crawled up her neck. "I just lost a dear friend of mine. And I want to uphold her memory as best as I can. I want to understand her."

"You want to write her biography? I don't know if I can sell something like that."

"It won't be a biography," Greta assured her. "More of a memoir of my own life, what she meant to me, and how our paths deviated." She stuttered. "I'll be talking about my years of exile, too. During the years Bernard was in prison. I know people are endlessly curious about that."

Cynthia brightened. "I've been asking you to write more about that for over a year. The answer was always no. Why the change of heart?"

"I need space and time to think about my life and my past and why things end up the way they do," Greta said with a sigh. "And the only way I know how to figure that out is through writing a book."

"Then it's settled," Cynthia assured her. "Let me know when you have pages for me to read. I can't wait to dig in."

There was silence save for the sound of a vacuum cleaner somewhere in the hotel.

"I'm sorry about your friend, Greta," Cynthia said.

"Thank you." Greta's throat was almost too tight for speech. "I loved her. But I'm beginning to question if I ever knew her at all."

* * *

The drive back to Nantucket was tense. Greta opted to sit in the back by herself, which meant that Alana turned around every half an hour or so to ask if she was all right. Greta wanted to scream back that she was okay. That she was always okay. But that was clearly a lie, so she said, "I'm not ready to talk about it. Can we leave it at that?"

It was a distraction to listen to Alana, and Jeremy talk up front. Greta imagined she was their ten-year-old kid, listening to her parents as they drove her home safely. Jeremy was talking about how beautiful Sarah's neighborhood was and how proud he was, and he choked up a few times as he mentioned memories he had of Sarah from when she was a girl. Greta empathized. It was heinous to watch your children move through life without you. At least he knew Sarah would come home for a visit soon.

Greta got home a little past two to find many of her grandchildren strewn across the beach in front of the house. Scarlet, James, Ivy, Rachel, Anna and baby Adam, Laura, and Danny were decked out in their swimsuits, stretched out on towels, applying suntan lotion, and listening to a speaker that played a song Greta had never heard and hoped to never hear again. She put on a pair of sunglasses and sat on the patio behind them, trying to distract herself with how happy they looked. Eventually, Scarlet noticed and popped up to beg her to come swimming with them. Greta couldn't think of a reason not to. She wanted to feel something besides this dull ache. She hurried upstairs to change into a swimsuit, then returned to charge into the waves hand-in-hand with Scarlet and James. James dove deep beneath the surface and came up twenty feet away from them. Greta's laughter echoed over the waves.

"How was the city, Grandma?" Scarlet asked, swimming over to her.

Greta treaded water. She was grateful for the strength of her muscles, grateful for a body that still hadn't failed her. Celeste had been in her forties. She should have had a resurgence. She should have had time to return to poetry and playwriting. It wasn't fair.

"Grandma?" Scarlet asked.

"You know how the city is, honey. You grew up there." Greta smiled and dunked herself into the water, where all she could hear was her own heartbeat. When she came back up, Scarlet looked at her with a mix of fear and curiosity. She wasn't used to Greta dismissing her like that.

"Sarah has a wonderful apartment," she said. "I think she'll be happy. We have to go see the play when it starts up."

"I'd love that," Scarlet said. She smiled in a way that proved Greta had fooled her into thinking all was well.

Was that another thing about getting older? Did you have to pretend to feel good all the time for the sake of everyone else?

Greta got out of the ocean and stretched out on a towel as her grandchildren frolicked. She knew someone was going to ask her what was for dinner soon. She wasn't sure she had the energy for it.

Suddenly, James started yelling. Greta burst to her feet and peered out at him. He was splashing and waving his hand. What was he saying?

"I found something!" he called again.

Greta's heartbeat calmed. Together with her grandchildren, she swam out to see what he had. On the sea floor was a very old anchor from a very old sailboat or smaller vessel. It was rusted and spoke of a potentially terrifying expedition. What was a sailor without an anchor? Lost.

"Should we pull it out?" James asked Greta.

Greta shook her head. "It belongs to the ocean, now," she explained. The ocean had swallowed it up.

Greta retreated to her kitchen to see what she could scrounge up for the grandkids. People padded in and out in various stages of clothing, swimsuits and towels. Everyone looked like a scraggly dog. Greta's heart swelled with love for all of them. It was the kind of love that would soon tip her over the edge. Before long, she'd have to hide upstairs and cry again. She was just so grateful for what she still had.

Greta agreed to meet Alana for lunch a few days later. Alana was pale and jittery and kept looking up from her menu to stare at Greta with confusion.

"You don't have to treat me like I'm fragile," Greta said. "I know I acted strangely in the city. And I'm not over it. But I'd appreciate it if you treated me normally."

Alana's shoulders slumped. The waiter arrived to take their orders. Greta went with the fish of the day and broccoli, while Alana opted for a salad with steak. They handed over the menus, and Alana tried to keep Greta's gaze.

"You don't want to talk about it?" Alana asked. "Some of the kids said you were really upset the other night."

"I lost someone I loved."

Alana furrowed her brow. "Who was Celeste Harding, Mom? I've never heard of her before."

"You should have heard about her. Everyone should have."

Greta knew she was being willfully obtuse, but she

wasn't sure how else to be. How could she come out and say it?

"I'm writing about her," Greta went on. "About the friendship we had back in 2003 and 2004. About the intensity of her mission to become a poet and playwright. And about why she might have failed." She shook her head as tears sprung to her eyes. "She was in Nantucket just a couple of weeks ago. We had coffee. I couldn't get over how strange she was acting. I felt like she was a shell of her former self. In reality, she was dying. Why didn't she tell me? She must have known I was judging her all that time! She knew me better than anyone for a while."

Alana gaped at her. Greta wasn't sure she'd ever shared so much of herself with her eldest daughter. The one who couldn't possibly understand.

"There's just so much I don't know about her," Greta said. "After she left Nantucket in 2004, I hardly heard from her until she sent me a letter last month."

Alana folded her lips. "She stayed at The Copperfield House in 2004?"

"She got here in 2003."

Greta watched Alana put together the pieces of this mysterious puzzle. *Everyone was trying to figure everyone else out all the time. It was impossible to fill in the gaps.*

"She was like a daughter to you, wasn't she?" Alana said quietly.

Greta crumpled into herself and stared down at the menu. It was painful to drop back into those old memories, painful to remember just how black her soul had been. "For a little while, we were all the other had," she answered. "I wanted so much for her. I got all of my real daughters back, thankfully. And it should be enough. But Celeste was like a lighthouse for me in the darkness. I thought I gave her everything I could. And then one day—she was gone. And I blame myself for her failure and, stupidly, the fact that she died so young. I have to understand what happened."

Alana sucked in her cheeks and watched Greta quietly for a few seconds. "You should talk to Ginny," she suggested, taking a notepad from her purse and writing down her phone number. "Maybe she has a clue of what happened to her after Winsome closed."

Greta took the piece of paper and placed it gingerly between the pages of her journal. "Thank you," she breathed, although she still felt lifetimes away from filling in the gaps. It was true that Ginny had heard through her network that Celeste had died. That put her in a better position than Greta, who'd known nothing at all.

# Chapter Eight

The Nantucket Sunrise Bakery was the number-one stop for Nantucket brides looking for gorgeous and scrumptious cakes. Alana had made an appointment with them to taste-test cakes the morning after Jeremy had proposed. Now, they were seated in the front room of the bakery before seven different cakes, all divine, with thick layers of frosting and little flower decorations and candy pearls. Jeremy had just taken a big bite of cake, which was terrible timing because the baker—Agatha Smith—had just asked him a question about his work in the Nantucket Records office. Alana laughed and touched his shoulder.

"He loves his job," Alana said. "But I think it's safe to say he loves this cake a lot more. It's going to be hard to choose!"

Agatha laughed. "If you can make this decision together as a couple, then you'll stay together forever. I'll leave you to it."

Agatha disappeared in the back and flipped on the

radio. Jeremy swallowed and turned pink. "That was embarrassing!"

Alana giggled and took a bite. It was in moments like these that she fully adored her life and had no regrets. She wasn't thinking about acting or about abandoning her dreams. She wasn't thinking about the wild, vibrant city she'd left behind. She touched Jeremy's leg under the table.

"I can't wait to shove one of these cakes in your face on our wedding night," Alana joked.

Jeremy cackled and raised a forkful to her lips. "Bring it on."

Outside, it was a beautiful afternoon in early June. Jeremy had taken a half-day off from work to indulge in "the best part of wedding planning." After this decision, they were nearly done. They would float through the summer and wed the final week of July.

"By the way," Jeremy said, "I haven't been able to stop thinking about what your mom said. Why do you think she wants to get to the bottom of what happened to Celeste? I can't make sense of it." He cut through the edge of his cake and held it.

"That's the way my mom is," Alana offered. "She thinks everyone has endless ambition. She can't under-stand when people don't meet their potential." She sighed. "Maybe it's the curse of being Greta Copperfield. She thinks everyone wants to be a famous artist. She thinks everyone wants to make literature, art or music that echoes the mysticism of the soul or whatever. And Celeste was apparently 'brilliant' enough for Greta Copperfield to get excited about. She blames herself. I don't know."

Jeremy cocked his eyebrow.

"What?" Alana asked.

"This question of meeting your potential is fascinating to me," he said, his voice quiet. "That's all anyone ever said to me when I was younger. 'You have great potential,' or, 'Your future is bright,' or, 'You're going to go far.' It felt like people tied up their own excitement about their life with mine. As though, if I really went on to play at Notre Dame and then professional ball, I was proving something about them because they believed in me first."

"People love to be involved in a story," Alana agreed.

Jeremy palmed the back of his neck. "It made me sick to disappoint them after the accident. Isn't that stupid? I was devastated, of course. But more than that, I couldn't look people in the eye. They were much more disappointed than me, and I couldn't bear to carry their disappointment." He shivered despite the heat of the day.

Alana squeezed his thigh as empathy rolled through her. She would always feel marginally guilty for that crash.

"I just wonder what will happen when your mother discovers a normal story behind all this," Jeremy went on. "Maybe Celeste decided she didn't want fame or glory. Maybe she realized that settling down and getting married and having children was enough for her."

"I don't know if my mother is capable of believing it," Alana said with a soft laugh. "But she's writing a book about it. Comparing her own life and failures to Celeste's. She'll project whatever meaning she wants to on what she finds."

Jeremy furrowed his brow. "You don't sound happy about that."

"My mother has an enormous capacity for emotion and creativity and truth," Alana offered. "But one thing she'll never forgive herself for is her twenty-five years of 'exile,' so to speak. I think she wanted to derive meaning from her own exile through Celeste Harding's success. And the fact that that didn't go to plan startles her."

Jeremy took another bite of cake and pointed at it with his fork. "This is the pinnacle of success for me. This cake. My beautiful bride. My wonderful and talented daughter." He smiled. "Losing that trip to Notre Dame was so painful. But it was also the best thing that ever happened to me. It gave me Sarah. It kept me here so I could meet you again. Life doesn't end when you're twenty-two."

"I felt so sure it would," Alana remembered. "That's what being a model was all about."

"But look at us now," Jeremy said. "Getting closer to fifty every day."

"And laughing in the face of it."

Even as Alana said it, her stomach seized with worry. If she was lucky, she had thirty years left. She spent thirty years showing the world what she was truly made of and proving to her mother that she was a sensational actress and a worthy performer. But no! She fought back against her own thoughts and took another bite of cake. She was getting married. Jeremy was right. There was such sublime happiness in acceptance.

Alana and Jeremy selected their cake, thanked Agatha, and stepped out to enjoy the rest of the day. They had dinner reservations for seven-thirty and decided to wander around and kill time and work up their appetites again. Downtown, they ran into Quentin and his wife, Catherine. Catherin was laden with bags from a boutique a street over, and Quentin was speaking enthusiastically about something.

"What's up?" Alana asked as she threw her arms around her brother.

"Quentin's all fired up about this new job," Catherine said with a smile.

"There's this inn on Martha's Vineyard," Quentin explained. "They've just discovered a hidden room in the basement. Nobody knew it was there. It belonged to the Underground Railroad!"

Alana's eyes widened. "That's incredible. You're filming there?"

"The History Channel reached out and asked if I wanted to be the face of the documentary," Quentin explained. "You should see this quaint little inn. It's called the Sunrise Cove. Just about the most romantic place."

"What does the room look like?" Jeremy asked.

Quentin considered this and shifted his weight. "It's about as creepy and damp as you're imagining it. According to our findings, an ex-slave raised her baby down there for over a year before the war ended, and she was free to live upstairs."

"It still blows my mind," Catherine said.

"What are you two up to?" Quentin asked.

"Nothing as exciting as that," Jeremy joked. "We just taste-tested seven different cakes. I'm so full!"

"That's equally important work," Catherine affirmed. "We can't wait for the wedding."

"Who said you were invited?" Alana teased.

"My sister never changes," Quentin said. "Always yanking me around."

Jeremy's phone buzzed, and he pulled it out to see Sarah's name. "She hasn't called in a few days. I gotta take this." He stepped away and answered it with a vibrant, "How is my actress doing in New York City?"

Alana watched him as his posture crumpled. She crossed her arms over her chest.

"Honey, I can't understand you," Jeremy said tenderly.

Alana and Catherine locked eyes. They knew what it was like to be a nineteen-year-old young woman weeping over the phone. They knew it meant disaster.

"Have you heard anything?" Catherine asked.

"Just that everything was going well," Alana whispered. "But things turn on a dime in theater."

"Especially in New York," Catherine agreed.

Jeremy got off the phone and staggered back to their little group. He was pale. Alana touched his shoulder and asked, "What happened?"

"She's had a few difficult rehearsals in a row," Jeremy said softly. "She's having trouble memorizing her lines. I think it's stress. Too much change at once." He touched the back of his neck and looked on the brink of tears. "I knew it was too soon. She's too young."

Alana's heart felt bruised. "It's just one bad day. It was bound to happen."

"She said she's been crying all week," Jeremy said.

Quentin and Catherine shifted uncomfortably. Nobody wanted to offer their opinion about Jeremy's daughter, who was so far away in the big city. Nobody wanted to parent anyone else's child. And it wasn't Alana's role, either. When she'd entered their lives, Sarah had needed her desperately; she'd needed help crawling out of the depths of her eating disorder. But she was better. She was going after something.

Alana was reminded of what Jeremy had said over

cake, that some people were just happier with normality. Some people discovered that settling down, having children and having a normal job filled them with enough purpose to keep going. Was Sarah one of them?

"I have to go see her," Jeremy sputtered. He looked resolute. "I'll call in sick or something."

"Let me go," Alana volunteered, surprising herself.

Jeremy looked stunned. For a brief moment, Alana thought he was going to say, *she's not your daughter; stay out of it*. But his face softened. "She would love that," he agreed. "You know that world better than me. You can see if things are as bad as they sound over the phone."

"I'm sure they're not," Alana said. "Sarah is an actress and a brilliant one at that. But actresses swing from one end of the emotional spectrum to the next. This will probably be just a blip in her memories by tomorrow."

Jeremy's face turned red. He glanced at Quentin and said, "I'm sorry. I must seem very foolish right now."

Quentin shook his head. "I have two daughters. Scarlet's all over the place, and Ivy's in her first year at college. I feel panicked just about every second about their whereabouts and health."

"You hide it well," Jeremy said.

"It's taken years of figuring that out," Quentin said.

"She'll be fine," Catherine assured them softly. She squeezed Alana's hand. "Let me know if you need anything."

"My recommendation is to bring her favorite snacks," Quentin said. "Something she can't get in the city. Something to remind her of home."

Jeremy thanked Quentin and led Alana to a wide range of Sarah's favorite snack places. He wanted desperately to bring her favorite ice cream in a big cooler filled with ice, but Alana talked him out of it. They opted for her favorite cookies with frosting, a specialty-made trail mix from a little shop downtown, and some black licorice —which Alana and Sarah adored and Jeremy thought was "the most disgusting thing ever invented by man." Back at home, they packed a bag with snacks and some trinkets that would remind Sarah that she was adored. Jeremy even wrote her a note that Alana didn't read. She imagined it said how proud he was, that he was always with her, that she could come home to visit whenever she wanted. His compassion for his daughter made Alana love him that much more.

Due to the frantic nature of the afternoon and early evening, Jeremy and Alana called the restaurant and rescheduled for a later date. Alana made them pasta with homemade pesto and parmesan, and they ate on the back porch, watching the water roll up along the sands. "I love you," Alana reminded him for perhaps the twelfth time that day. "I love you back," he said.

# Chapter Nine

It was a total surprise to hear that Alana was headed back to New York City so soon. Greta read the text message on the back porch and immediately called her to see what was up. "Sarah is having a hard time," Alana explained. "I'm going to go check on her."

"A hard time?" Greta asked.

Alana sighed. "It's her first time away from home. I think she's freaking out."

Greta leaned back in her chair and felt the last rays of the dying sun across her cheeks. She considered the fact that Ginny still hadn't returned her phone calls that week. Maybe Alana would tease Ginny out of whatever hideaway she was in. Maybe that way, Greta could get information out of her.

"Can I come with you?" Greta asked.

"Really?" Alana sounded doubtful. It was true that Greta and Alana didn't see one another one-on-one this often. Greta more often met with Julia one-on-one, as she was her literary daughter and more apt to have a dialogue about books and writing.

"I love being back in the city," Greta said. "And wouldn't you like the company? It's a long drive."

Greta waited for Alana on the front porch the next morning with her suitcase tucked beside her. Alana appeared around the corner seven minutes later than she'd said, and Greta hurried to throw her suitcase in the back and clamber in. Alana looked frantic. "Jeremy is just so worried about Sarah. I want to handle everything so he doesn't have to take work off. But she's his baby. His only."

Greta took a deep breath. It surprised her to see Alana aching with empathy and fear like this. It was clear she loved Jeremy deep in her bones.

It wasn't till they boarded the ferry that Alana asked, "So, Mom. Why did you really want to come to New York?"

Greta raised her eyebrows. "Why do you ask it like that? As though my motivations are sinister?"

Alana sipped a cup of coffee and raised her shoulders. "Not sinister. I just know you're trying to learn more about this Celeste woman. Did you discover something? Something that's pulling you back?"

Greta sighed and shook her head. "Ginny never got back to me. I want to go through the library archives. They have a theater division. I'm hopeful they have information about the Winsome Company and what happened to the people involved in their latter productions."

Alana brightened. "I'm heading to rehearsal as soon as we get there. I'll ask Ginny if she can meet for dinner tonight. I'm sure she's just been too busy to call you back. Sarah says rehearsals have been grueling."

Greta bit her lip. "I hope it isn't too much trouble?"

"Ginny loves showing off the restaurants and bars she knows and loves," Alana reminded her. "Even if she doesn't have any information to share, I'm sure we'll have a great night together. And it'll be good to take Sarah out and make sure she's well-fed and happy. It's been just a week in the big city, but I'm sure it's felt like a thousand years."

Greta remembered when she'd first reached Paris as a young woman. She'd felt far away from anything she knew or understood; her thoughts were incoherent; she'd spent the third afternoon holed up in her room, sobbing. Little did she know that Bernard was waiting just a few streets away. Little did she know she'd walked into her future.

The drive to the city breezed by. Alana and Greta talked about easy things like swapping memories from a time of goodness and joy in the Copperfield clan. Sometimes, Greta wondered why she and Alana had never gotten along. This gorgeous woman was charming! A dream! Greta probed her own memories to try to make sense of it but came up dry. Families were inexplicable.

Alana dropped Greta off at the public library near Central Park. "I'll send you details about dinner," she promised before adding, "I love you. Good luck!" She whipped back into traffic and was surrounded by a wide variety of horns. Greta smiled, turned, and walked up the library steps. The library was guarded on either side by massive stone lions. It gave the experience a regal feeling. She wasn't in Nantucket anymore.

A woman in spectacles at the front desk guided Greta to the theater department's archives. "The city has hosted more than one hundred theater companies over the past forty years," she said as they walked down the stairs. "But we've kept a record of just about all of them. Theater people tend to want to document things like that. They help."

Greta thanked the woman and stood at an enormous filing cabinet filled with records and documents regarding theater production companies from the years 1977 to 2024. She flipped through several ones she knew for a fact had produced her plays—during the eighties and early nineties, mostly, and reminisced about coming to the city with Bernard to see the productions. She'd held her breath throughout each play. She hadn't been able to believe that people had put so much work into the strange things that poured out of her brain.

Before long, she returned to her Celeste Harding quest and pulled out documents regarding the final years of Winsome Theater Company. Because they'd disbanded in 2008, there were plenty of photographs that offered a direct view of what it had been like to be a part of the troupe. Celeste was in the middle of several, smiling prettily, carrying scripts around. According to one of the files, Celeste had written eight plays for the troupe and directed four of them herself. Greta's heart swelled with pride.

Greta thought back to the summer of 2003. Celeste and Greta spent several weeks writing a script. Celeste came up with a few plot points, and Greta adjusted them slightly until they had a wonderful plot. After that, they wrote by speaking lines in the air on the back porch of The Copperfield House. These were happy times for Greta. She burned with creativity all the time and frequently woke up in the middle of the night to record what she'd been thinking. It was impossible how quickly the two of them had written that script. But when it was over, they spent a beautiful afternoon splitting the parts and acting it out. Celeste had tears in her eyes as it finished. "This is really something special, isn't it?" Greta hadn't known if Celeste meant the play or their time together at The Copperfield House. She'd burst into tears, too.

That was the same day Celeste told her about growing up in her parents' house. Her father had been a drunk; her mother had often left and come back again. They'd fought almost constantly when they were together.

It was then that Greta realized that she was Celeste's mother figure. Greta never left Celeste. She never left The Copperfield House. She offered a beautiful and stable environment for Celeste's creativity to grow and prosper.

"You're going to be something special, Celeste Harding," Greta had promised her. "I can just feel it."

Alana texted to meet her, Ginny, and Sarah at a French restaurant on the Upper West Side. Greta wandered through the greenest Central Park she'd ever seen, watching baseball games and eating an ice cream cone until it was time to meet. Greta got to the restaurant before the three of them but said simply the name "Ginny" and was led to the perfect outdoor table. Alana, Ginny, and Sarah floated toward her soon after that like a dream.

Ginny extended her arms to hug Greta before the others. "I'm so sorry, Greta! I keep meaning to call you back. We've been positively overwhelmed with rehearsals. This play needs a lot of work. I'm not speaking of Sarah when I say that. The director hired a few actors that I probably wouldn't have. Raw talent, for sure—but untrained!" She shook her head as she sat across from Greta.

Greta smiled at Sarah and looked for signs of distress on her face. But Sarah smiled confidently back.

"She was brilliant," Alana answered before Greta had a chance to ask. "Absolutely stunning."

"Whatever." Sarah flipped her hair.

"Not whatever," Ginny assured her. "You've got both raw talent and experience. You're a force to be reckoned with. Pete..." She glanced at Greta to add, "Pete's the director. Pete said he didn't need to see anyone else for that role after you auditioned."

Sarah melted on the spot and turned her eyes to the menu. She looked ravenous. Alana would tell Greta later that Sarah had spent all night weeping but woke up excited because she knew Alana was coming.

They ordered white wine for the table. Greta held herself back from jumping all over Ginny with questions about Celeste. When the waiter came with their wine glasses and a bottle, he poured it gingerly and talked about the regions of France from which the grapes were taken. Greta didn't even listen. Finally, Ginny turned her eyes to Greta, bowed her head, and said, "I want to answer everything I can about Celeste. Ask whatever you want."

Apparently, Alana had filled Ginny in a bit about Greta's mission. Greta's cheeks were warm. But she couldn't stop now.

"I was just in the theater archives reading about the plays she wrote and directed for Winsome," Greta said.

"She was sensational," Ginny said. "It wasn't that long ago, but women weren't necessarily directors and playwrights as often. Things have changed like that." She snapped her fingers and looked at Sarah as though trying to impress her.

"She must have been sad to see Winsome go," Greta suggested.

"We all were," Ginny said. "I didn't get work immediately after that. I floundered, but I wasn't the only one. But Celeste got work right away. I believe she was writing for a company called Handel. She was writing a brand-new play for them. It was all quite exciting."

Greta furrowed her brow. Why did she feel devastation coming?

"I think she was nearly done with the play when everything changed for her," Ginny went on.

"What happened?" Greta asked.

Ginny blinked with surprise. "I'm sorry. I thought you would have known that, too. Ginny's mother came to the city in 2010. But it was short-lived. She died by suicide about two months after she moved here. It completely destroyed Ginny, obviously. She quit working on the play and took a leave of absence from the company. Somebody else slipped directly into the place she left behind."

Greta gaped at Ginny. "That's horrible."

"Yeah. I was hanging out with her a lot right before her mom came," Ginny went on. "She was really apprehensive about her mother moving here. Said that she'd always given her a lot of trouble. I don't think she had a cozy upbringing. But the minute her mother arrived; Ginny seemed right as rain. She wanted to make up for lost time. One time, I even joined them for a picnic at Central Park. They were laughing and making up silly songs together. I felt like I had joined their secret club."

Greta blinked away her tears. "Did Celeste tell you anything about why she might have taken her own life?"

"I didn't see Celeste after that," Ginny confessed. "The funeral was in Celeste's hometown rather than in the city. She didn't come back to the city for a while, and she stopped taking my calls. That was the same story for just about everyone."

Greta filled her lungs and considered this beautiful and creative Celeste coming up in the world of theater. To lose your mother was a horrific thing. But to lose her by suicide added dimensions. There was always worry with suicide that you'd been the one to push them over the edge. Greta's heart shattered around the edges.

"I guess that's all I can really tell you," Ginny said sadly. "I wish there was more."

"Me too," Greta offered.

"Maybe I can hook you up with a few other members of the troupe," Ginny suggested. "Most of them have already left New York. They gave up." She laughed softly. "But I have most everyone's contact details."

"That would be fantastic. Any information is worthwhile," Greta said.

The waiter returned to take their order. Greta ordered her favorite French dish—chicken a la orange, which she'd made for a young Celeste numerous times. Celeste had scraped her plate clean and always asked for more. She'd been so alive.

# Chapter Ten

Greta was able to chat with three other members of the Winsome Theater Troupe that week on the phone. They were all keen to regale their times in New York theater and frequently got off-topic so that they could brag about the soliloquies they still had memorized or the difficult costume changes they'd managed in fifteen seconds flat. They all remembered Celeste fondly. One of them had briefly dated her during 2007—before a crushing breakup that had nearly forced him out of the troupe. "But Celeste demanded I come back to rehearsal. She wouldn't hear of having our 'silly breakup' destroy my career," the man named Reggie said with a laugh. "I still loved her. I guess I never really got over her."

"Were you surprised when she left the next troupe and quit writing altogether?" Greta asked.

"She was reeling about her mother. I knew that she had a really difficult relationship with her," Reggie went on. "They didn't speak for the entire time I dated her, but she cried about it sometimes. She felt she'd done something wrong. That she'd abandoned her mother when she should have stuck up for her in the face of her father."

"He was a drunk, right?" Greta asked.

"Worse than that. It sounds like he sometimes hits her mother," Reggie went on. "Celeste didn't like to talk about it, but she mentioned it a few times."

"Did Celeste's father ever hit her?"

Reggie was quiet for a moment. "She never said if he did or not. But she knew violence. She knew trauma."

"What makes you say that?" Greta hunted through her own memories for times Celeste might have mentioned something traumatic that had happened. But her mind's eye produced only gorgeous sun-dappled memories of herself and Celeste on the back porch writing and running lines. It was as though she'd blocked out everything dark about that time.

"I can't help but feel like I'm betraying her by telling you this," Reggie went on.

Greta cocked her head and adjusted her phone on her ear. In her quest to discover Celeste's past and paint a clear picture, she'd never once thought of it as a betrayal.

"I think it's good to understand her better," Greta said tentatively. "I think she'd want us to know her totally."

"I don't know if that's true," Reggie said. "She had many secrets. I don't know if she ever told anyone everything. She was a writer; that was how she worked through her problems."

Greta's stomach twisted with fear. Was Reggie going to keep a piece of the puzzle away from her? Did he not trust her with it?

"She always talked about the darkest time of her life," Reggie finally went on. "It must have been 2002 or so. She was on the road, traveling from place to place. She'd always thought it would be romantic to be a vagabond, the way everyone does when they're young. She said she met people who weren't kind. People who taught her about the cruelty of the world."

Greta frowned. 2002 was the year before Celeste had stomped up to the door of The Copperfield House like a straggly dog.

"I don't have anything to back this up," Reggie added tentatively, "but I think there was a man involved. An abusive man. I don't think he ever hit her; I think she said she got away before he could. She was amazed to have fallen directly into a relationship modeled after her parents."

Greta had been taking notes on a pad of paper. She circled the words "abusive man on the road" as though that could be the secret to everything. But there was so little she understood. She thanked Reggie profusely.

"She meant a lot to me," Reggie said. "I was sad to see her leave New York."

"When was the last time you saw her?"

"It must have been a few months before she married her first husband," Reggie went on. "I ran into her near Broadway. She told me all about her wedding preparations. She seemed about as excited about it as any play she'd ever written. I was amazed. I'd always imagined her to be this free spirit who would never settle down. But I suppose we all need a place to lay our heads."

"Especially someone like Celeste," Greta offered. "Someone who didn't have a place to live for so long."

Greta said goodbye to Reggie and leaned back in her office chair, clicking the end of her pen. Whoever this abusive man was, Celeste had left him in her past. Greta liked to believe that she'd helped her through that process here at The Copperfield House. She'd filled Celeste's plates with nourishing food, given her creative and stimulating conversation and allowed her to shuck off the horrors of the past for a little while. But history always repeated itself. Was it possible that Celeste had met someone similar to that man in the years after her mother's suicide? Was it possible she'd declined rapidly after doing so much work to build herself back up?

It was nearly five-thirty. Greta went downstairs to prep dinner for herself, Bernard, Julia, and the members of The Copperfield House residency, both past and present. Aurora was coming by with her boyfriend, Brooks, and the videographer, poet, and sculptor currently residing at the residency planned to discuss their projections with Bernard and Greta that evening after dinner. She'd promised them exquisite French food. She decided on chicken a la orange.

Bernard stepped into the kitchen a few minutes after she started and set to work chopping veggies for a salad. He'd had a stimulating work session that afternoon and was in a wonderful mood, teasing Greta and kissing her on the back of the neck. Greta beamed at him.

"There's something wrong," Bernard said as he studied her. "What is it?"

Greta set down the big meat cleaver and rolled her sleeves up over her elbows. "It's Celeste. An ex-boyfriend of hers mentioned an abusive ex she'd mentioned. But I don't know how to get to the bottom of that story. It feels like taking one step forward and two steps back."

Bernard snapped his fingers. "Didn't you say that Celeste was sent here by an older brother? A writer?"

Greta felt the lightbulb go on in her head. "I'll check the records!"

Greta left Bernard in the kitchen to check the computerized records of every single artist, writer, dancer, filmmaker, and so on that had ever stepped through the doors of The Copperfield House residency. This had been a task she'd assigned James late last summer. He'd computerized everything for ten dollars an hour. Now, all she had to do was type "Harding" into the search bar and draw up the file immediately. Brad Harding had been at The Copperfield House during the spring of 1995—eight years before Celeste had darkened its door. There was a photograph of him as a young man, confident and brash, and there were a few writing samples from his time at the residency. Greta vaguely remembered him. She hadn't liked his writing as much as another writer staying with them at the time, and she'd probably unfairly spent more time with the other writer and left him in a lurch. A brief Google search told her that Brad had published three novels with mid-level success. He was in his fifties and lived in Providence, Rhode Island. Greta immediately contacted his literary agent and asked for his email address. By the time she was finished cooking dinner, the agent had written back.

Greta felt lost in a dream during dinner. As she blinked around the table, listening to the artists and family members she loved dearly exchange stories, talk about their projects, and exclaim about how good the food was, she felt transported through all the decades of life and artistry at The Copperfield House. It seemed incredible that, at one time, it had only been her and Celeste at the house. They usually hadn't dined at the table like this and opted for the kitchen because it was cozier with just the two of them. But on Christmas, they'd eaten here, taking up as much space as they could and listening to romantic classical music. Had Celeste been harboring a recent secret about an abusive ex-boyfriend? Why hadn't Greta seen it written on her face?

Aurora helped Greta clean the table and wash the dishes. Greta adored Aurora, a woman who'd come to The Copperfield House last summer and suffered a complete breakdown after working herself half to death. Her mother had also been a resident at The Copperfield House. But now that Aurora was in love and on medication, she was bright and happy; her creativity wasn't bound to destroy her. She even showed Greta a few paintings she was working on, which Greta gushed over. Aurora was a success story of The Copperfield House. She was one of the reasons Greta wanted to keep going.

It took Brad Harding three days to answer Greta's email.

*Greta,*

*Thank you for your email and your touching comments about my little sister. I knew she'd stayed at The Copperfield House for a brief period, but I didn't know you knew her as well as you did. Back then, Celeste and I didn't have a very good relationship. It improved with time.*

*You say you have questions about my sister. I can't imagine what they could be. But here's a suggestion: I'm going to Martha's Vineyard with my wife next week for a brief vacation. Perhaps we could meet and discuss this more. I'm happy to come to Nantucket.*

*All the best,*

*Brad Harding*

Greta wrote back that she would take the ferry to Martha's Vineyard on whatever day he had time. He was already coming all the way here; she might as well meet him.

Brad suggested meeting at the Aquinnah Cliffside Overlook Hotel. It was a swanky new resort-style hotel on the cliff that catered to elite vacationers. Greta took the ferry and drove out to Aquinnah, where she parked and stepped inside. Brad was seated by the window with a book in front of him. She tried to guess what it was as she approached. Something hefty and pretentious like Joyce or Dostoyevsky. But she was surprised to find he was reading Doris Lessing instead. She immediately warmed to him.

Brad glanced up, offered a half-smile, and stood to shake Greta's hand. Greta remembered saying goodbye to him on his last day at The Copperfield House. "I wish you good luck in your career," she'd said. But she hadn't actually anticipated he would become much of anyone, not like his sister.

"I love Doris Lessing," Greta said as she sat down. "She's sensational."

A waiter came by to take their orders. Greta was jittery and ordered a white wine, while Brad opted for a Diet Coke. Greta guessed he was sober; alcoholism ran in their family.

"Thank you for meeting me today," Greta said. "I'm sorry to interrupt your vacation. I'm sure you need it."

"I usually take the afternoons to read anyway," Brad said. He tapped his fingers across the table. "And like I said, I'm curious about your friendship with my sister. She never mentioned you."

Greta's heart felt bruised. "I met up with Celeste three weeks ago. She was in Nantucket and asked to get coffee. She didn't mention her illness at all."

"Would you want to talk about it all the time?" Brad asked. "It was all her family and friends could fixate on. She probably wanted to pretend that everything was all right."

Greta wanted to point out just how dull their conversation had been. But she thought that maybe that played into Brad's theory, too. Celeste had wanted to have a normal everyday conversation with someone she'd once loved, Greta. And Greta had spent that time judging her. Her stomach roiled. When the wine came, she drank it too quickly and shivered.

"I've been trying to put together the pieces of Celeste's life," Greta went on. "We spent a very intense year and a half together, and I hardly heard from her after she left The Copperfield House."

Brad raised his eyebrows. "She stayed with you for over a year?"

Greta felt a jolt of pride. She'd offered that young woman safety in a world that seemed so cruel to her. "Yes."

"She never mentioned that," Brad offered. "I assumed that she stayed as long as any artist did during my time there. I had a room for about three or four months if I remember correctly."

"Three months was typical back then," Greta said. She cleared her throat and added, "You've done very well for yourself, Brad. It's always wonderful to see an ex-Copperfield House resident take their career so seriously."

Brad raised his shoulder. "I don't remember you being quite so enthusiastic about my work back in 1996."

Greta faltered. He remembered the way she'd regarded his work, too. Her thoughts raced for a way out of this. A way to prove that she adored his writing if only to get him to tell her more about Celeste.

But Brad waved his hand and gave her a half-smile. "I've gotten way better since then. If anything, your reluctance to give me praise was the drive I needed to take myself more seriously. I didn't publish a book till 2003, but I wasn't ready till then, either. But I was impatient. Probably arrogant." He smiled. "I'm still slightly arrogant. I don't know if that ever goes away."

"You have to be a bit arrogant to publish anything," Greta said. "It's the nature of writing."

It was less tense between them. Greta loosened her shoulders. "I met someone by chance who knew Celeste in the city," she went on. "She talked about her tremendous years at the Winsome Theater Company. That was after her year with me. I was so pleased to know she'd had so much success there." Greta furrowed her brow. "But I didn't know about your mother until very recently. I'm so sorry that happened."

Brad turned and looked out the window at the jagged cliff that jutted across the property. "Celeste and I went many years without hearing from our mother. It was a surprise to us both when she popped up in New York wanting to build a relationship with Celeste. I was in London at the time, touring my first book, but I called Celeste when I could. I was terrified that something bad was about to happen."

"What made you think that?"

"Because in our family, something bad was always about to happen," Brad said. "It felt like we were cursed. But Celeste continued to reassure me every time I called. She said that Mom was better. That she was stable. That she'd gotten a job and an apartment all on her own. She sent photographs of them together at Central Park, picnicking and smiling. They looked just like any other mother and daughter.

"Celeste called me the day after Mom died," Brad went on. "She sounded so flat. So tired. She reminded me of our mother when she went through her depressive spells when we were kids. It took me forever to get it out of her that Mom had died by suicide. I wasn't surprised. Like I said, she'd been depressed for most of my childhood. The fact that she'd had Celeste as an older mom hadn't helped things. I'm pretty sure Celeste was a mistake or a mad dash for Mom and Dad to fall back in love again. Who knows? I urged Celeste to seek help, and I made arrangements to come to the city to help. By the time I got there, Celeste had already quit the new theater company. We traveled back to our hometown and buried our mother in her family plot."

"Did you stay home long?" Greta asked.

"About three weeks," Brad said. "There were loose ends to tie up. There wasn't an inheritance, of course, but we had to sell the house and get rid of all the stuff Mom had left behind when she'd spontaneously gone to New York."

"Did Celeste talk about going back to the city? Did she talk about wanting to keep writing?"

Brad hesitated. "I remember she talked about wanting everything to slow down for once. I told her that was possible. She could write from anywhere; she didn't have to live in the fast-paced city."

Brad's eyes filled with tears, and he put his hands over his face as his shoulders sagged. Greta kept herself from reaching out to touch him on the shoulder. It wasn't appropriate. He wouldn't have liked it.

His words were tear-soaked. "I think we thought the worst was over after that. Our father was dead. Our mother was gone. And we could carry on with our lives as writers and artists; we could be better than they ever were." He smeared his fingers down his cheeks and added, "But for Celeste, that wasn't the end of her misery. It was really only the beginning."

Greta gaped at him for a long time, waiting. Outside, dark clouds roiled over the island and threatened to shake them with a sudden storm.

# Chapter Eleven

Alana woke up on the futon in Sarah's studio apartment. Birds twittered out the window, and Manhattan sunlight pierced the glass. Her phone said it was only six-thirty in the morning, but Sarah had to get up and get ready by seven-thirty. It was a day that called for bagels and heaps of coffee. It was a day that called for reminding Sarah just how much she mattered in the world, that she was needed, and that she needed fuel to start her day.

This was Alana's second visit since Sarah moved in, a result of Sarah having called her sobbing yesterday morning. "I'm just having a really tough time." Alana had told Jeremy she'd go right away. The truth was far more complicated, of course. She'd become addicted to the wild Manhattan days and nights, to the smorgasbord of restaurants, to Ginny's stories, to the daydream of whatever life she might have had if she hadn't followed Asher all over the world and become his sad wife and fallen apart shortly thereafter.

It was mid-June and already seventy-five degrees. She

took a key and slipped down the street to get two every-thing bagels with scallion cream cheese and two massive coffees. When she returned to Sarah's apartment, Sarah sat at the end of her bed and rubbed her eyes.

"Morning, sleepy head!"

Sarah winced and took one of the coffees. "Thank you." She sipped it and winced again. "I'm so sorry about yesterday. I feel like such a little kid."

"Don't worry about it! I'm happy to be here." Normally, Alana stayed at a hotel, but she'd opted for Sarah's futon last night because they'd stayed up late watching films, eating snacks and chatting. Alana thought, *if this is what it means to have a daughter, I'm all in.*

They'd also run lines for more than two hours. Sarah felt stumped as to why she struggled to learn lines in the city alone. "When you're here, it's like they stick in my head better," Sarah had said. Alana's heart swelled with love. It was so nice to feel needed.

It reminded her of all the years of her life when she'd tried to make Greta feel not needed. She regretted it.

Sarah and Alana ate bagels and talked about the day ahead.

"I asked Pete if you can sit in on rehearsals," Sarah said. "He's cool with it."

"Really?" Alana was surprised. Ginny had said that Pete, the director, liked closed rehearsals and that he didn't want to give away any of his secrets before he was ready.

"Yeah! But you'll get bored," Sarah said. "They last forever."

"I won't get bored," Alana promised.

These proved to be famous last words. Morning

rehearsal lasted from eight-fifteen to one-thirty, and Alana was too terrified to stand up and distract anyone by opening the door to leave. She threw herself into watching and listening, but there were only so many times she genuinely appreciated watching the same scene. Pete was at times enthusiastic and at other times pulling out his hair. Alana wondered if he was acting out what he thought a typical director should be like. Maybe it was all fake.

When morning rehearsal broke, the lights came on overhead. Alana was surprised and blinked wildly. The actors jumped off the stage and hurried out to grab lunch before their afternoon rehearsal began. Sarah sidled up to Ginny and spoke to her quietly. Alana felt like a sore thumb. Was she invited to lunch? Should she just slip out quietly and let the actors do their thing? She'd told Sarah they could get burgers after and just hang out. That's what she was here for.

Pete turned and looked at Alana. His eyes were penetrating. After a split-second, he dropped his folder on stage and strode toward her. Alana felt cornered. Was he going to tell her that he wanted her out of rehearsal? That this wasn't meant for her?

"I know you," he said when he got close enough.

It sounded like an accusation. Alana blinked at him.

"I swear I do," Pete went on.

A smile crept over Alana's lips. She shifted her weight and popped her hip out to one side. It was rare to be looked at like this. Like she mattered in a city of eight million.

"Have we met before?" Alana asked.

"I don't think so," Pete said. "But I know I would have

liked to meet you." He snapped his fingers. "Where have I seen that face?"

Alana arched her eyebrow. "I'm Sarah's stepmother. Well, almost."

Pete seemed not to have heard her. He stepped closer and narrowed his eyes. "You were in Times Square."

Alana's heart dropped into her stomach. "Just once."

"For ages," Pete said.

Alana remembered how eerie it had been to see her face in Times Square as big as a mountain, how she'd smiled down on everyone and felt like the queen of New York.

"But that wasn't all you did. I remember you in commercials. And magazine ads."

"I was on the cover of Vogue," she said.

Pete snapped again. "You were everywhere, baby."

Alana laughed with surprise. In a city as fast-paced as New York City, she hadn't imagined anyone would remember her days of modeling.

"I was in love with you for years," Pete went on.

Alana was incredulous. "Based on my advertisements?"

"They weren't just advertisements," he said. "They were magic."

Alana was floored. She tucked a curl behind her ear as he continued to stare at her. She'd forgotten what it was like to be looked at like this. She'd forgotten how much she missed it.

"That's very kind of you," she said.

"I'm not kind," Pete assured her. "But I know when someone has it. And baby, you have it."

Alana laughed again and squeezed her fists. She wasn't sure what to do. "I'm in the city for a few days.

Maybe you want to join Sarah and me for dinner one night?"

"Sarah's a real talent, too," he said. "I adore her."

"So do I." Alana breathed out.

"Dinner sounds fantastic. Why not?" Pete pulled his phone from his pocket to check his calendar. "I can do tomorrow night."

"Perfect," Alana said. "I'll pick you up here."

After that, Alana turned on her heel and sauntered up the auditorium aisle. She didn't have to look back to see Pete staring after her. A shiver ran down her spine. A director had just told her she had "it." But what did that mean for her career?

Pete's eyes were dangerously flirtatious. But he knew Alana was Sarah's soon-to-be stepmother. She'd said it right out of the gate. But this was how these director guys were. They wanted to stake ownership over you. They wanted to win.

Alana had to be very careful with him. She had to keep him at a distance.

But what if he wanted her to perform for him? What would she do then?

Sarah was excited that Pete planned to join them for dinner tomorrow. "He never hangs out with anyone from the production," she said. "What did you say to him to change his mind?"

Alana laughed. "He recognized me from my old modeling days. Isn't that silly?"

They were in line to get burgers. Sarah didn't look surprised. "I've met a few people who remember you from those days," she said. "I don't think I fully knew how influential you were."

Alana wanted to say she didn't either. But she

decided to keep that to herself. She had to increase her own mystique.

"You were really good today," Alana said.

Sarah winced. "It's so strange that I remember all of my lines when I know you're close by."

"Does that mean I have to go to every single performance, too?" Alana asked with a laugh.

"I'll get over this soon," Sarah said sheepishly. "I'm sorry."

Alana touched her shoulder. "You don't have to be embarrassed. This is normal. It's your first big gig in the city! I imagine your nerves are all over the place."

Sarah nodded and let her smile drop. "I hope Dad isn't upset that I keep calling you here."

"You know how he is. He gets plenty of time to watch his TV shows, movies and sports. There's nobody there to nag him to eat healthily. It's a dream."

Sarah laughed. "Not that we're eating healthily either!" She reached up to take the tray laden with greasy burgers and a pile of home-cut fries.

"Don't tell your father," Alana quipped.

Alana stayed at a hotel that night to give Sarah some space. She sat at the bar for a little while with a book that she hadn't read and instead googled her old advertisements from her modeling days. Not everything was online, but some were. She was careful not to let anyone see that she was looking at gorgeous and glossy photographs of herself from nearly thirty years ago. She felt a stab of fear. Every minute that passed, she got further from that young woman. She had almost nothing in common with her anymore, save for the fact that people like Pete remembered her.

Alana called Jeremy that night. He answered on the

second ring. "How are my city girls doing?"

Alana laughed and stretched languidly on the bed. "Your daughter is doing so well."

"That isn't what she says when she calls home and begs you to come down."

"I think she's just going through growing pains," Alana said. "You should have seen her in rehearsal."

"They let you into rehearsal?"

"They did," Alana said proudly. "And the director even remembered my old silly advertisements from back in the day."

"You're kidding."

Jeremy had told Alana numerous times that seeing her face plastered everywhere after they'd broken up had nearly driven him insane. She hoped talking about it now didn't bother him.

"It's silly," Alana affirmed.

"It's not. And it makes sense. You were brilliant in those ads," Jeremy said. "I can't believe I get to marry the famous model Alana Copperfield. I hope the city doesn't take you away from me."

Alana felt a tug on her heartstrings. "Never. I love you."

"I love you, too."

Alana spent the morning in the hotel spa. It was luxurious and freeing. She sat in a piping-hot sauna, closed her eyes and imagined all her pores opening and clearing. Sometimes, she pictured herself on her wedding day in just six weeks; other times, she imagined herself center-stage on Broadway as Pete directed her down below, his eyes narrowed. She always shook that image out.

Alana picked Sarah, Pete, and Ginny up from rehearsal at seven-thirty that evening. Ginny had nabbed them an exclusive table at a Thai restaurant in Greenwich Village. The other members of the cast eyed Sarah and Ginny enviously. They probably wondered if this meant that Sarah and Ginny's performances were better than theirs. They probably assumed they wouldn't be selected for Pete's next production.

The world of theater was cut-throat. Alana knew that it was rare to feel a director's light shine upon you like this.

The night was beautiful. Gorgeous New Yorkers swarmed Greenwich Village and wove in and out of bars and restaurants. A guy around Pete's age approached and shook his hand. "We worked together years ago," he said. "I hope you're well?" Pete played along until he left. Then he turned to whisper in Alana's ear, "I don't know that guy at all. I wonder what it's like to be so washed-up that you cling to old memories like that?" Alana laughed nervously. It felt wonderful to be a part of Pete's world and his little jokes.

It reminded her momentarily of what it had felt like with Asher. He'd been so important. So widely known. But when she'd been the only one in his orbit, her life had felt truly golden. He'd only shared his secrets with her.

They sat at the restaurant and were immediately served cocktails and small plates of Thai appetizers. Pete was talking to Ginny and Sarah about the production in a way that made Sarah's eyes sparkle. Alana smiled even though she didn't know what was going on. This was Sarah's moment! Her time to shine!

"So," Pete said as he stuck a small toothpick into a dumpling, "you're going to be Sarah's stepmother. That's it, right?"

Sarah nodded excitedly. "The wedding is at the end

of July."

"Coming up quick," Pete said.

"It doesn't interfere with any of our performances," Sarah promised.

Alana smiled wider but couldn't help but feel that Pete was scrutinizing her. As though he wanted her to say something cross about weddings or Jeremy.

"Weren't you married to someone very famous?" Pete asked.

Alana kept herself from rolling her eyes. "All things come to an end."

"But who was it? It wasn't Asher, was it? That sniveling guy." Pete laughed. "It was. I can see it written all over your face."

"It's over now," Alana said. She couldn't tell if Pete was flirting with her or toying with her or both. She'd been out of the game too long.

Sarah grabbed Ginny's elbow and said, "Look! Felicity is here!" She waved at a woman in the corner who was also in the production. "Let's go say hi."

Ginny and Sarah popped up to say hello to Felicity. This left Alana alone with the provocative Pete. She filled her mouth with water and looked directly past his head at the street outside the window. She knew he was going to say something, but she couldn't guess what.

"I can't believe you quit," Pete offered.

Alana parted her lips with surprise. Of everything, this was probably the worst thing he could have said. "I had to go back to Nantucket," she said. "My marriage broke up, and my father got out of prison. It's a long story."

"I skimmed some of it in the news," Pete said.

Alana was momentarily flattered that he'd googled

her family. She hated that she felt that way. But there it was.

"And now you're getting married," Pete went on, "which means your career is really over."

"I wouldn't say that. People get married all the time."

Pete's eyes glinted. "Is that so? You're going to auditions? You're planning?"

Alana remembered the high school girls she taught back at The Copperfield House. She adored them so completely. If she left to pursue her own career, who would be there for them? That wasn't to mention Jeremy.

"I might have a few auditions in the pipeline," Alana said. Why was she lying to this man!? What was wrong with her?

"Good. Fantastic. You must audition for my next production," he said.

Alana was taken aback. She remembered what Ginny had said of Pete after the more recent auditions, that he'd told her she was basically a shoo-in. Was this conversation proof that Alana was a shoo-in, too? She shifted on her chair but kept her smile even. She was accustomed to this from years of modeling; she'd always known how to manipulate the camera to keep it interested in her. She had the same effect on Pete.

Pete removed his phone from his pocket. "Give me your number."

Alana flinched, took the phone, and typed in her details. By the time she handed it back, Ginny and Sarah were on their way to the table. Their laughter echoed through the restaurant.

"I can't wait to see what you're capable of, Alana Copperfield," Pete said just before they sat back down. "I've been dying to know for almost thirty years."

# Chapter Twelve

It was June 21 and the morning of the Summer Solstice. Greta woke up at five to go to her office to pore over the notes she'd compiled for her current manuscript—a memoir that wove together Celeste's devastating losses with Greta's own. A memoir that hoped to analyze the devastating reality of humanity alongside its quest for truth, beauty and art. What Brad Harding had told her last week had invigorated her creative process and brought another level of sorrow to the picture. She could still hear Brad saying, *"But for Celeste, that wasn't the end of her misery. It was really only the beginning."*

According to Brad, Celeste had already met her first husband by the time her mother died. His name was Marshall, and he was a firefighter in Manhattan between the years 2003 and 2010. He came from a long line of firefighters, including a father and grandfather who both lost their lives on September 11, 2001. Marshall wore his trauma on his shoulders like a jacket.

Greta wrote, *Brad doesn't know how Marshall and*

*Celeste met. He thinks it has something to do with a fire on another level of Celeste's apartment building. Based on police records, that would have been at the end of 2008— around the time Winsome Theater Company closed its doors for good.*

"Celeste was always curious about people," Brad had told her. "Even as a kid, she would go up to people and ask them questions about what they were doing or wearing or eating. She was always adorable, and later, she was beautiful, and people opened up right away. I imagine she walked right up to Marshall when he was in his firefighter uniform and asked him what was up. And how could a firefighter like Marshall resist someone like Celeste? She was charming, unique and creative. She had a wonderful way with words."

"What did you think of Marshall?" Greta had asked.

"I thought he was a brute. Just like our father. She never confessed that he hit her, but I wouldn't have been surprised."

Greta wrote, *Celeste married Marshall six months after her mother died and moved to New Jersey. Brad remembers her saying that she was done with New York and done with theater. He figured it was just a phase, that she would come back to the theater when the time was right. But not long after she married Marshall, they started trying for a baby.*

"I couldn't believe she wanted a baby right away," Brad had said. "I didn't want to say anything, but it seemed obvious she was trying to fill the hole our mother had left."

"I think that's a common reaction to something so difficult," Greta had said.

Brad was quiet for a long time before adding, "But it was another step toward her ruin."

Greta wrote, *Celeste got pregnant right away and called her brother to share the news. Brad was nervous; he didn't like Marshall and wanted her to leave him when she found the strength. He knew that a baby would complicate things. But after his wife's urging, Brad went over to Celeste's with flowers and chocolate to congratulate them. Everything was right as rain that afternoon. Marshall doted on Celeste, and Celeste spoke about the baby in absolutes. But not a week later Celeste called him sobbing. She said she'd had a miscarriage. Brad reminded her this was really common, that women lost babies all the time. But she just kept saying, "Not like this. Not like this."*

"She was so fragile," Brad had said.

"What do you think she meant by 'not like this'?" Greta asked.

"I've thought about that often," Brad said. "My only guess is that Marshall did something to cause it. Maybe he hit her. Maybe he upset her so much that her hormones went out of whack. I don't know. But the next thing I knew, I couldn't get a hold of Celeste. I called her house three or four times a day. If Marshall was there, he just let it ring and ring. I was terrified. I went over there to see her, but Marshall told me she'd gone out of town. This didn't seem likely. He had red-rimmed eyes, and he slunk around the shadows of their house like a ghoul. Finally, I told him I was going to call the police and suggest he'd done something to her. He looked at me with these tiny evil eyes and said, 'She went to the looney bin.' I couldn't believe he'd said it like that."

Greta wrote, *Marshall drove Celeste to the hospital three days after her miscarriage. She couldn't stop crying.*

*Eventually, they checked her into the mental institution attached to the hospital to keep an eye on her.*

Greta's heart felt pulpy. She stopped typing and looked over her notes again. It felt strange to put together the pieces of this puzzle from so long ago. And she hated picturing Celeste's beautiful face so crumpled and sad like that. Celeste had needed her mother so desperately during that time.

Why hadn't Celeste reached out to Greta? Would Greta have been receptive? Would she have come to her aide? She liked to think she would have. But her past was as foggy as the Sound in autumn.

Greta glanced at her phone and stood with a start. She had twelve missed calls and ten messages from Julia, Scarlet, Ella, Laura, and Alana. The realization hit her all at once that she was late for Alana's bachelorette weekend. She flung herself through the office door and got ready in five minutes flat: makeup, hair, swimsuit, summer dress. She and Alana had more or less mended their not-so-great relationship—and she didn't want to destroy all that progress like this. She had to get to the harbor as soon as possible.

Greta parked near the harbor and hurried to find the Copperfield women in a buzzing group near the dock. Alana wore a funny white veil that Sarah had brought her from the city, and the others wore pink t-shirts that said, "Alana's Crew." Greta was surprised at how easy it was to laugh after all she'd learned about Celeste. Scarlet tossed her a t-shirt, and she put it on over her white tank top.

Greta hugged Alana and whispered, "I'm sorry I'm running late!"

"It's okay," Alana assured her. "We were worried when we didn't hear anything from you."

Ella swung her arm around Greta's shoulders and said, "None of us live with you anymore. We couldn't come bang on your door."

Greta's heart swelled at the memory of the nearly two years that her children had lived with her and Bernard again. Their children had taken up every room of the house, and conversations could be heard from every room and every hall. She made a mental note to write about this time of her life one day, a time during which she'd learned the true meaning of being a grandmother and opened her arms to all these darling creatures who wanted to love her back. Maybe she'd get to it after the Celeste memoir.

Julia had rented a sailboat for the day. It was big enough for all the Copperfield women who'd agreed to come along: Greta, Alana, Julia, Catherine, Scarlet, Ella, Laura, Anna, Sarah, and Ivy. Just before they pulled the anchor up, they spotted another Copperfield-adjacent family member hurrying down the dock. It was Eloise, Greta's little sister. Greta hadn't seen her in a couple of weeks, and she threw her arms around her and felt like a girl again—before the dark realities of adulthood had grabbed hold of her—if only briefly.

They set out for the glittering waters. Alana and Julia were both passionate sailors, and they handled the sails and the vessel easily as the others situated themselves like cats in the sun. Scarlet handled mimosas and passed out buttery croissants as Ivy set up a speaker system to play a perfectly cultivated playlist of all of Alana's favorite songs. Sarah sat next to Greta with her mimosa and clinked her glass with Greta's.

"How does it feel to be back from the city?" Greta asked.

"I cried when I got back to my room last night," Sarah

confessed. "Dad had bought all my favorite snacks, and he wanted to stay up late watching TV together and talking during commercial breaks. I ended up falling asleep on the couch like a little kid."

Sarah looked beautiful, a woman who knew she was on the verge of conquering the world, one theater production at a time. Greta felt as though she basked in her glory.

"But it sounds like it's going well?" Greta asked.

"Better than that," Sarah said dreamily. "I told Alana I would stop begging her to come to the city as often to take care of me." She laughed.

"I don't think she minds," Greta said. "You know we're always here for you. You're already an official Copperfield in my book."

Alana turned to look at Greta and smiled knowingly. Greta remembered when Alana ran off with Asher to New York City; she'd hardly ever called home or told anyone what she was up to. Greta had spotted her eldest daughter in a glossy magazine—as a model—and nearly fallen to her knees. Her thoughts had been all over the place. On the one hand, she was thrilled that her daughter was making it work in one of the cultural hubs of the world. On the other hand, she hated that Alana wasn't using her brain—and instead just her beauty—in a world that would soon turn its back on her when she aged up.

But Alana hadn't been the sort of young woman to listen to reason. And she definitely hadn't called Greta, crying and begging her to come visit, unlike Sarah.

Alana dropped anchor near a beautiful cliffside, and Julia announced it was time for lunch. Alana sat across from Greta, and the wind teased her veil gently. Greta, Julia, and Ella set about brunch preparations, laying out hummus and fresh bread, dried Italian tomatoes, all sorts of cheese, eggs, sausage, and adorable cakes. Greta could have eaten everything twice; it was just that good. Scarlet went around to refill mimosas as Julia suggested they play a game for the bachelorette.

"No!" Alana begged. "We don't need to play any games."

Julia gave her a secretive smile and tugged out a big folder. "I spent some time working on it. I think you're going to like it."

Alana blushed and rolled her eyes as the others twisted to see what Julia had.

"The game is 'Guess What She's Selling,'" Julia explained. "I have here twenty-five different advertisement campaigns that Alana modeled for. I've taken out the advertisement copy, and it's up to us to guess what in the world she's supposed to be selling based on the photograph."

Alana's face went slack for a split second. Greta was the only one who noticed. The others exclaimed with excitement.

"I haven't seen enough of your stuff, Aunt Alana," Ivy said. "And I've always wanted to."

Julia arched her brow at Alana. "Do you mind? I think it'll be fun. And you're so good! These photos are stunning."

"Fine," Alana said. Her laughter rang false. "Go ahead. I probably don't remember half of what they advertised."

Julia clapped her hands and brought out the first photograph. In it, Alana wore a nightgown and a gorgeous pout. They'd done her makeup with smoky dark eyeliner and eye shadow. "Guess what she's selling?"

They went around the circle. Scarlet guessed, "That nightgown," while Ivy went with, "Eye shadow." Catherine said, "Night cream," while Ella said, "I'll go with something weird and say sleep medication."

When it came time for Greta, she said, "It's an advertisement for singles who want to go on blind dates."

Julia's eyebrows rose. She was quiet for a moment. "That's it," she said. "How did you know?"

"I remember it," Greta said. "It must have been spring of 1999."

Alana was captivated. "You saw it? Do you remember what magazine it was in?"

"It must have been People," Greta said. She could practically still feel the magazine in her hands.

"That's one point for Mom!" Julia said.

Alana continued to gaze at Greta. She was shocked. But Greta went on to win the game outright. Out of twenty-five, she guessed thirteen correctly. The only person who got close was Ella. It seemed that advertisements had changed a great deal since the late nineties and early 2000s, and the younger girls didn't stand a chance.

Immediately after the game wrapped up, Scarlet took off her clothes to reveal her black bikini and leaped into the water. Anna joined her a few seconds later and laughed as she came back up. She didn't look like a young woman who'd lost her fiancé and was now raising a baby with her new boyfriend's help. She looked light and free and easy. *There's so much you can't know about a person. So much that they hide.*

"Come on in, Grandma!" Ivy called.

Greta laughed and waved her hands. "In a minute."

When she turned around, she found Alana directly beside her with a freshly poured glass of mimosa. She looked as though she had no interest in swimming. "I can't believe how many of those you got right."

Greta raised her shoulders. "I didn't have a whole lot else to do but pay attention to your modeling career."

Alana flinched, and Greta immediately regretted having said it. She didn't want to belittle Alana's career in the slightest. She wanted to be a better mother than she had been; she wanted to mend this.

"I was fascinated with it," Greta offered after a pause. "And I wanted to see your face so much. I hated that they put so much makeup on you. I wanted to see my daughter as she was."

Alana blinked back tears and took a sip of mimosa. The other Copperfield women leaped from the boat so that only Alana and Greta were aboard.

"Can I tell you something?" Alana asked quietly as the others hollered and yelped.

"Of course you can."

Alana sighed and cast her eyes across the horizon. "Sarah's director recognized me from my modeling days. He wants me to audition for his next production."

"Really!"

Alana couldn't suppress her smile. It was clear that this pleased her even though it complicated everything. "I don't know what to make of it. On the one hand, I'm thrilled to be getting married again, and I'm head-over-heels in love with Jeremy. On the other hand, I never felt like I had reached my potential by acting before my life fell apart. I've been heavy with regrets. And this feels like a window to the world I always wanted to join." She sighed. "Ginny has made me so jealous over the past few weeks. I've wondered so often what could have been if I'd never left New York. If I hadn't gotten so involved with Asher. If I hadn't given up."

Greta wrapped her arm around her daughter's back. It was rare for the two of them to share such intimacies.

"And now that you've spoken so much about Celeste and her 'failure,' so to speak, to reach her potential, I can't help but wonder if I should be doing more," Alana went on. "Maybe that's stupid. But this life is the only one I have."

Greta nodded. "Have you talked to Jeremy about this?"

"I don't want to scare him. I will never leave that man. Not unless he leaves me first. But I can't help but think I have to go after this, just to see what happens."

"You absolutely do," Greta said. "And Jeremy will move mountains to help you do what you want to do. He loves you without question. He'll be in the front row on opening night and probably every other night thereafter. You know that, right?"

Alana smiled and dropped her head on Greta's shoulder. "I know you're right. But I'm also worried telling him about it will jinx it. I hope the director hasn't forgotten. Maybe he says this sort of thing to women all the time. Maybe it's a manipulation tactic."

"I don't think he would ever lie about wanting you to work for him," Greta affirmed. "Didn't you see those advertisements? You're a star, honey. You've always been."

Alana laughed. "I was in my early twenties. Everyone is a star in their early twenties."

"That's not true, and you know it," Greta said with finality.

Scarlet hollered from down below for Aunt Alana

and Grandma to join the fun in the water. Greta and Alana laughed and stripped down to their bathing suits. They hovered at the edge hand-in-hand and counted to three before they leaped in together. Greta swam into the chilly depths and then burst up, rubbing her eyes of salt. The sun shone upon them, and their wet hair glinted. She wasn't sure the last time she'd felt so free.

That night, Julia booked them for dinner and drinks at a swanky restaurant on the coast. Alana was the guest of honor at the head of the table, and Greta grabbed a chair a few away from her, between Julia and Ivy. They all ordered fish dishes and Spanish-inspired tapas, plus glasses of wine. The conversation bubbled. Everyone was saying everything at once.

Alana tapped her glass with a fork delicately until the table quieted. "I'm sorry to interrupt," she said. "I just want to thank you all for this wonderful party. It's been a dream to hang out with you all day on this gorgeous Solstice. Sometimes, I don't know what to do about all this love I have for my family." Alana caught Greta's gaze and smiled. "Thank God that we all came back to Nantucket. It's where we belong."

# Chapter Thirteen

The next morning, Greta was back in her office with the tiniest of post-wine headaches. Bernard had told her to relax and take a break, but it was already June 22, and she'd promised to have the first draft of her novel ready by autumn. That didn't give her much time.

Greta continued her work from yesterday by writing, *according to Brad, Celeste was in the mental hospital for two weeks before she was released. Brad made sure to be at Marshall and Celeste's place when she arrived home. He wanted to intimidate Marshall, he said. He wanted to make it known that Marshall couldn't hurt his sister and get away with it. But Celeste looked so happy to see Marshall. She hardly left his side and continued to talk about the babies they would soon have and the bright future that awaited them.*

Brad had said, "She was on some kind of medication that dulled her senses. An anti-depressant or something. I wasn't sure that was the right thing, either. She had to experience her grief after our mother's death! She had to recognize that Marshall was no good! But when I told her to take care of herself, she took my hand and said, 'Don't worry about me, Brad. I'm going to be a mother soon. I'm going to be fine.' My wife was begging me to go home, and I had another book due that year, and everything felt frantic. I feel as though I let Celeste slip through the cracks. But before I knew it, she was calling to say she was pregnant—for real this time. She'd waited four months to share the news. I was thrilled for her, to a point."

Greta wrote *Celeste had her first child in early 2012. A boy. Marshall was thrilled.*

Brad had said, "What you have to understand is that Brad lost his grandfather and father to 9-11. He wanted to extend his family's line. He wanted a little boy who would eventually turn into a firefighter. But when the baby was six months old, he became very sick. He had to be hospitalized for more than a month. This destroyed Celeste all over again. When I saw her next, she was a shadow of her former self. She was doing everything in her power to keep her little family afloat. That was the day she told me she was pregnant again. I told her she couldn't handle it, that she had too much on her plate. She needed to get back to writing if she was ever going to! But she just shrugged her shoulders as though I was taking everything too seriously."

Greta wrote, *Celeste's son survived his illness. At the beginning of 2013, she had another child, a daughter. She was lonely at home, and Marshall was not a worthy partner. Brad assumes he had affairs, but he never confirmed anything. By the end of 2013, Celeste was back in an institution. Brad and his wife picked up the slack with her children because Marshall called them sobbing. It was around that time that Marshall packed up everything he owned and fled. They never heard from him. And when they finally broke the news to Celeste, she was so out of her mind with grief that she was required to stay in the institution for another two months.*

It was hard for Greta to align her previous memories of Celeste with this other Celeste. She opened another document on her computer and began to write about a memory she had of Celeste. They'd written another play together during January, February, and March of 2004, one that Greta actually thought would have a long life in New York City if Celeste ever dared to take it there.

"But you can't put my name on it," Greta had said as they washed dishes late one night. "It has to be you and only you."

Celeste scoffed. "What are you talking about? We wrote this play together. I'm going to credit you. And who says I'm ever leaving Nantucket anyway?"

Greta turned off the water and looked at Celeste with her eyebrows raised. She thought, *It's true that it will kill me when Celeste leaves. But I can't keep her here. I have to push her out so that she achieves what she needs to achieve. I have to let her know how essential it is to go after your dreams.*

Greta said, "I'm washed up, Celeste. I'm nothing. You're going to be the great one. You're going to go the distance."

Celeste rolled her eyes. "You're not washed up. You're fifty, for crying out loud. You could keep up your sensational career if you wanted to."

Back then Greta felt a wave of anger roll through her. She turned back on the water and thought about Bernard alone in a cell somewhere. She wanted to scream and cry and break the plate in her hands. But she couldn't. Carrying on like that wouldn't help.

Brad had given Greta Celeste's second husband's contact details. Until now, Greta had refused to contact him because he recently lost his wife and the mother of his two children. She didn't want to bother him. She didn't want to drag him through the sorrows of the past. Of the husband, with whom Celeste had been vacationing in Nantucket in May, Brad had said, "She met him in late 2014. She was working as a copywriter at a little advertising agency in her town of New Jersey, and he was their accountant. I think she liked the stability of him. That, and she really wanted a father for her children. It terrified her to do it alone."

Greta had said, "I can't imagine raising children alone. I can't blame her."

And again, she'd cursed herself for ever thinking less of Celeste Harding on that final day she'd ever seen her. There was so much Greta hadn't understood.

It was a surprise that Celeste's second husband, Greg, wrote back within the hour.

"Greta, thank you for your kind message about my wife. We miss her dearly. We would be happy to welcome you to New Jersey any time that suits you. It sounds like you had a wonderful relationship with Celeste, and I'd love to learn more."

Greta arranged to go to New Jersey on July 1st. Until then, she fixated on the notes she'd taken during her conversation with Brad and outlined how her story might align with Celeste's in her memoir. She sent a rough outline to her agent, who said, "OH! I love this. Keep going." Greta didn't need the boost. She planned to keep going regardless. She was obsessed.

Things at The Copperfield House carried on in much the same way. The current artists in residence left during the last week of June, and they held a final party for them to say goodbye and wish them well. Bernard made a final speech that brought tears to Greta's eyes. He spoke about their unending commitment to the arts and just how important the arts were for empathy in this world that so often misunderstood itself. That night, Greta cuddled against Bernard before they fell asleep and watched the moon float dreamily out the window. She thought, *How many years did I sleep in this big house all by myself? How many years did Bernard sleep in his prison bed alone? Yet here we are together, building our dreams side-by-side again. Why was I so lucky? Celeste was so unlucky. She lost her life.*

Alana was jittery about her upcoming audition for Pete, the director. Twice, she confessed she still hadn't told Jeremy about it. "Every time I sit down to tell him, I end up talking about something else. I'm totally terrified to audition, and I know he would be completely in my corner. It's like a mental block I can't shake." Greta decided to give her daughter a pass. It was clear she was battling all sorts of emotions: fear of the unknown, fear of what she'd already lost, as well as apprehension, anger and embarrassment for going after her dreams. Greta said, "If you get the role, you'll have to tell him. And like I said already, he'll be over the moon."

It just so happened that Alana's audition was to be held on July 2nd. Greta made arrangements to stay in the city on July 1st so that she could meet up with Alana after the audition and hear how it went.

"I'll probably be a mess," Alana warned her.

"Then we'll grab a wine and forget about it," Greta assured her.

Greta was so anxious about her interview with Greg that she decided to leave Nantucket on June 30th and stay at a hotel in a New Jersey suburb. The hotel was located twenty-five minutes from Celeste's old house, stitched between two fast-food restaurants. Greta considered taking a swim to calm down, but the pool was clustered with screaming children, and she padded back upstairs and removed her suit. She wasn't sure why her interview with Greg filled her with such doom. But she felt she was getting closer to understanding Celeste and what had gone wrong. And she ached for Celeste almost all the time.

It felt as though she carried her ghost with her.

Greta woke up early the next morning and grabbed breakfast at the little diner attached to the hotel. She ate eggs, vegetarian sausages, and a biscuit slathered with butter, then scrubbed herself clean in the shower, dried her hair, and headed to her car to drive to Greg's. She had to drive a few times around the block so as not to arrive too early. She didn't want to surprise Greg and the kids too early. Plus, she wanted to remember Celeste's children's names. Greta remembered how earnest Celeste had been about her children, talking about her son's desire to be an accountant and her other son's perfect attendance. She'd taken refuge in the lives of her children rather than building her career.

The minute Greta rang the bell, a boy opened the door and blinked at her. He was maybe twelve and Celeste's eldest. He gave her a look of confusion and called, "Dad!" Greta's heart warmed at the thought that Greg had adopted both of Celeste's children from her marriage with Marshall. He was probably a fantastic guy—even if he was an accountant. Or maybe all accountants were fantastic guys. They were certainly stable. They didn't have the arrogance that came with many artists, musicians, and filmmakers. They woke up every morning, made their breakfast, cared for the people in their lives and went to bed on time. They carried life without needing to advertise just how painful it was for them. But that was the thing; being alive was inherently painful. Accountants, too, felt it. They just didn't feel the need to carry on and obsess.

A middle-aged man with graying hair rounded the hallway corner with a toddler on his hip. He smiled a tired smile as he approached and extended his hand. "You must be Greta. I'm Greg."

"Who are you?" the twelve-year-old asked.

"I'm an old friend of your mother's," Greta offered, feeling uneasy. How could she say that she was actually a friend when she knew so little of Celeste's real life? "I was the friend she visited on Nantucket in May."

Greg furrowed his brow. "I'm sorry?"

Greta immediately felt she'd done something wrong. "On May 14th. I met with Celeste at a French coffee shop in Nantucket. By the harbor." She cleared her throat. "Celeste mentioned she was there with you."

"We were there together," Greg offered. "But she didn't mention you or any coffee shop."

Greta's heart felt bruised. The twelve-year-old was looking at her accusatorially, and she wondered if she should just leave. Celeste hadn't even wanted Greg to know about her existence six weeks ago! Was Greta breaking that trust?

"Sorry," Greg offered with a wave of his hand. "My

emotions are all over the place. Come in. Please." He beckoned and then shut the door behind her. He then put the toddler down in front of the television and gestured toward a messy kitchen. "Can I get you a tea or a coffee?"

Greta shook her head. She didn't want to make this young single father do more than he already had to. "You have a lovely home."

"It's a mess," Greg said with a laugh. "I always knew Celeste was cleaner than me, but now it's for real. I hope one of the kids grows up to be really organized. Maybe I can bribe them to keep the house in order." Greg smiled. "Why don't we talk in my office?"

Greta followed Greg down the hallway and into a plain office with white walls and a long white desk that looked like it was from IKEA. Greg closed the door behind him and sat in one of two office chairs, gesturing toward the other. There was a photograph on the wall of the entire family—four children and Greg and Celeste. Celeste looked like the version of herself Greta had met in May.

"It's incredible to meet you," Greta began, although she wasn't sure she believed that. She would have much rather met Celeste at a gorgeous Michelin-star restaurant in the city and heard about Celeste's success as a playwright and director.

"You as well," Greg said, but only because he was polite. He fluffed up his hair. "I wonder what day Celeste said you would be in Nantucket. It must have been the day I played golf with a man I met at a restaurant. But I can't understand why she wouldn't have told me."

"Where did she say she was going?"

"She wanted to rest and catch up on reading," Greg

said. "She didn't have much energy at that point. She was napping almost all of the time."

Greta's heart thumped. "Was it her idea to go to Nantucket?"

"It was," Greg said. "It came out of nowhere. She suggested that she stop the chemo and all the medicine because it wasn't going anywhere anyway. She wanted to enjoy her last months on earth. We went and got her a really lovely wig, and..." Greg paused and pressed his hand over his mouth. Greta was sure he was about to sob.

"She lived in Nantucket for over a year," Greta offered. "With me."

Greg's eyes bugged out. "When?"

"In 2003 and 2004," Greta said. "She came out of nowhere on a stormy night and didn't leave for ages. She became sort of an adopted daughter for me. I was very lonely at the time." Greta swallowed the lump in her throat, surprised that she'd already told Greg so much. "After she left for the city, I hardly heard from her until May when she said she planned to come to Nantucket."

Greg's eyes sparkled with intrigue. "You don't think she planned the trip to Nantucket in order to see you one more time, do you?"

"I'm sure it wasn't me," Greta lied. "I know she just wanted to spend a beautiful week with her husband." She swallowed. "She spoke so fondly of you and the children. I had never seen her as a mother."

"She was a brilliant mother," Greg affirmed. "It was a role she was born to play."

Greta's heart pumped. She went quiet as her thoughts hummed too quickly for her to make sense of them.

"You said you were working on something about my wife. That you needed information?"

Greta returned to herself and took a breath. "I've been trying to make sense of Celeste's brief yet wonderful life. When I met her, she was just about the most dynamic and interesting writer I'd ever met. But when I saw her in May, she didn't mention playwrighting at all. I've wondered ever since then why she gave it up."

Greg's lips parted. He gaped at Greta for a long time before saying, "Playwrighting?"

It was as though Greta had said "alien invasion" or "gluten-free bread."

Greta nodded. "She was brilliant. I know she worked at a couple of theater companies in the city before her mother died. After that, she moved to New Jersey. I'm curious about her work after that. Maybe she wrote without showing it to anyone? Maybe she found artistic merit there?"

Greta leaned forward, and the office chair creaked beneath her. She threatened to throw her to the ground. Greg's face was difficult to read.

"I'm sorry," he said after a long pause. "I don't know anything about that."

Greta's heart pumped. "But you know about her playwrighting career. You must have read her work. You must know how brilliant she was."

Greg palmed the back of his neck and looked out the window. He looked like a man who'd just discovered a new continent but planned to turn back and not tell anyone about it. "She was a copywriter when I met her," he said, which was information Greta already had. "I knew she was brilliant at that. I knew she was much better than that advertising firm. But she had two children, and we were falling in love. There was no talk about 'going after your dreams in the city' or anything like that."

He grimaced and looked Greta dead in the eye. "I'm sorry. It's bizarre to learn this new facet of someone I'm mourning."

Greta understood in her bones. Greg was probably trying to figure out why Celeste had kept so much information from him. Maybe she hadn't thought he was worthy to know? Or maybe she'd wanted to shove all reminders about that time of her life into the back corners of her mind?

There was no telling what it meant. But Greta saw, clear as day, that she'd broken Greg's heart. And that hadn't been her plan.

"I should go," Greta said. "I'm really sorry to bring this on you. It wasn't my intention."

Greg sputtered and stood up. He looked on the brink of crying. "She never mentioned writing fiction to me," he said as he wrung his hands.

"Did she ever do anything creative?" Greta asked because she couldn't help herself.

"She painted with the kids sometimes," Greg said. "But she always talked about how terrible she was at it. We both were."

Greta looked at the door and considered running out of there, away from this beautiful family and their tremendous pain.

"None of our kids are that creative either," Greg went on. "One of them wants to be an accountant."

"Celeste told me that day in Nantucket," Greta said. "She was really pleased about it."

Greg raised his shoulders. "What does it mean?"

"I think it means that making art brought her tremendous pain," Greta said after a brief pause. "I think it means she didn't want her children to go through that.

And she never wanted to bring that darkness to your home. Not with you here."

Greta frowned. She hadn't expected this truth to fall upon her like this. But here it was. And it made a great deal of sense.

Greg walked Greta to the front door and opened it. Celeste's eldest son watched her like a hawk as she prepared to go.

"She was a wonderful mother," Greg said again. "I don't think she ever wanted anything else."

"I'm sure you're right," Greta said. "Thank you for your time. The world has lost a wonderful person. It will never be the same."

After that, she swept from Celeste's home, and her four children and her very sad husband stepped into her car and sped to the city. She cried the entire way.

# Chapter Fourteen

Alana woke up in her Manhattan hotel on the morning of July 2nd with the worst kind of headache. It rattled through her and pressed her into the mattress. Tears sprung to her eyes. When she regained a bit of strength, she crept up and poured herself a massive glass of water as her heart pounded. *What was this? What had she done to deserve this?* And then she remembered. Today was her audition with Pete, and she still hadn't told Jeremy. Maybe this was her subconscious mind forcing her to pay for keeping the truth to herself. *That isn't how you start a marriage.*

She hadn't told anyone about the audition except for her mother. As she filled her mouth with chilly water, her mother texted to say:

"Break a leg."

Alana's heart swelled. She knew that her mother respected going after your dreams above all things. In some ways, Alana recognized that she was auditioning to prove something to her mother. But she never would have admitted that. Not to anyone.

Alana went for a brief run through Central Park, showered in the walk-in shower, put lotion all over her body, then dressed in a pair of black jeans and a black V-neck t-shirt. It made her look slightly sultry and slightly younger than she was—both benefits in the audition room, which is something she'd learned more than half her life ago. At ten-thirty, she struck out for the Broadway stage, where they were holding auditions. Sarah had mentioned that Pete's assistant director was holding her play rehearsal today because "Pete is already thinking about his next project. He's obsessed!" Ginny's eyes flashed then, too, and Alana wondered if Pete had already spoken to Sarah and Ginny about his next project. Maybe they were both "shoo-ins" for autumn. It wasn't hard to envision herself in their midst by then—an actor in her own right on an off-Broadway stage.

Alana reached the waiting room for the audition and immediately shriveled up with surprise. She'd presumed that everyone auditioning would be around her age—forties, at least, but she found that most of them were in their twenties or early thirties (with good anti-aging tactics). Most of them knew each other and laughed and talked about parties they'd recently attended. It reminded Alana of her long-ago days of modeling and her brief foray into acting. She'd known everyone back then, too. But not now. She was a nobody now. She sat in the corner and went over her lines again, realizing that it was far easier to remember the lines from Sarah's play than this one. She supposed that was because it had been so nourishing to rehearse a play with someone else. She'd done all of this on her own.

And she'd mostly kept it a secret—which felt so isolating.

"Who are you auditioning for?" A woman beside her asked. She looked to be in her late twenties or early thirties and wore a dark brown bob and a pair of big glasses that looked like they were from the seventies.

"Martha," Alana said. "And you?"

"Same. Martha." The girl smiled wider as though she were relieved. She was going up against this much older woman. It was clear to her that Alana wasn't "real" competition.

Alana's cheeks burned. But she didn't want to let this younger woman get in her head. "Have you worked with Pete before?"

"No. But a friend has," the young woman offered. "I've met him a few times. He's a dream."

"Totally," Alana said before burrowing herself back in her script. All she wanted in the world was to be transported out of this room and back into the home she shared with Jeremy in Nantucket. She wanted Jeremy to pop his head in and ask, *Should I make popcorn for the movie?* She wanted to be able to breathe again.

But a few minutes later, Pete's assistant called her in for the audition. Alana walked like a woman about to jump off the plank of a pirate ship. She entered the dark theater and found herself stage-centered, with lights burning down upon her. She could just barely make out Pete and a few others in the audience. She forbade herself from saying hello and being chummy with Pete. In reality, she hardly knew him at all, and she didn't want to seem silly. She took acting seriously.

"This is Alana Copperfield reading for Martha," the assistant called.

This was Alana's cue. She cleared her throat and began a monologue that Martha's character says halfway through the play—immediately before a miscarriage rattles her future and ultimately causes her husband to leave her.

"This baby is our everything," Alana said, gazing out across the black seats, imagining that they were filled with hundreds of people in a future audience. "It's what we've always wanted. The other morning, Zach woke me up, placed his head on my belly, and listened. I knew he could hear her talking to him. I knew that our baby was telling him secrets that she didn't even share with me. And I knew we would be the kind of family who refused to acknowledge our past. We're future people. We're headed for a new dawn."

The monologue went on a little bit longer. After that, Pete acted as Alana's husband in the play, and Alana answered him perfectly. Her embarrassment, fear and shame at trying to do this at such an "old" age fell away, and she was completely and totally the character. By the end of the scene, she was fully crying. She was that immersed.

In the end, Pete, his assistant, and the three other people who sat with Pete observing the audition stood up and clapped long and hard. Alana blushed and touched her cheek. The lights went up, and for a moment, she was genuinely surprised that nobody else was in the audience.

"That was incredible, Alana," Pete said. He walked to the stage and pressed both of his palms on it as he gazed up at her. Alana felt like some kind of goddess. "Really. You should have seen some of the garbage that walked on this stage today."

Alana laughed nervously. She couldn't get rid of her smile. Over and over again, she thought, *this is it. I've done it. My acting career is off to the races again.* And then, *But how will I tell Jeremy?*

"Thank you, Pete," Alana offered. "And thank you for pushing me to audition. This was really fun."

"Fun is exactly what it should be," Pete said. "But you didn't look like it was fun. You looked totally immersed in the character. Truly amazing."

Alana smiled wider, and Pete heaved himself up onto the stage and sauntered toward her. Alana again was reminded of Asher, of the sort of arrogant artist-type who wanted to "own" you." She took a hesitant step back and hoped he didn't notice that she was frightened of her. That would only make his pursuing her more enjoyable for him. And she did not want to be pursued!

"I genuinely can't imagine anyone better for this part," Pete went on. "I should send everyone else away."

"Don't do that," Alana said. "The next Nicole Kidman is probably out there."

"Really? Oh dear. Send her away first," Pete joked.

Alana raised both eyebrows and laughed nervously. Did Pete think Nicole Kidman was a bad actress? Was he insane?

"We should talk later this week," Pete offered.

"Sure! Yes. Of course," Alana sputtered. "We really should."

"I just have so many ideas about this production and about your character in particular," Pete went on. "Maybe we can talk over dinner about it on Friday?"

Alana's thoughts pounded. Friday was July 5th, which was one day after the Fourth of July, which probably meant she would be spending endless days with the

Copperfield family, eating hot dogs and swimming in the sea. But Pete's eyes were gleaming with such certainty. How could she turn down this opportunity?

"I'm sure I can work it out," Alana offered.

"You'd better," Pete said. He gently punched her upper arm. "Get ready for your real life to begin, huh?"

After that, he turned and swung back off the stage. "I'll text you the details," he called behind his shoulder. His assistant led Alana off the stage and called the next woman for her audition. Alana slunk back into the overwhelmingly bright July afternoon and pressed her hand across her heart. *What was that?* She thought. *What on earth did I just get myself involved with?*

But she didn't have long to spiral. She planned to meet her mother for lunch at two p.m. on the Upper West Side. Alana walked through Central Park on her way to the restaurant, pausing several times to draw her cheeks up and into the sun. *In a few months, I'll be able to do this all the time,* she thought. *Maybe Jeremy could take a leave of absence from work and come to the city with me. Maybe everything can work in my favor. Maybe Jeremy would even fall in love with New York and suggest living there part-time for Sarah and Alana's careers.*

But already she heard Jeremy's voice saying, *What would I do in New York? My job is here in Nantucket. Why would you ever assume I wanted to go to New York City and do nothing but be your husband?*

It wasn't clear if he actually would say that, but she could feel it bubbling beneath the surface.

Greta was already seated at their table when Alana arrived. She was hunched with her elbows up, looking far less ladylike than Alana had seen her maybe ever. Her eyes were to the ground and rimmed red. Had she been crying? Alana hesitated and fixed her face. She didn't want to launch into news of her audition too soon, not if her mother was going through something.

But the minute Alana reached the table, Greta pulled her head up and asked, "How did it go?"

Alana's smile was instantaneous. "I think it went really well." She dropped into the chair across from her mother. "I don't want to jinx anything. But he wants to meet to discuss the character later this week. I don't remember that ever happening when I was in my twenties. I think it must be proof that I'm a better actress than I was twenty years ago, you know? I've been teaching these girls for a couple of years. Maybe my teaching rubbed off on me." Alana laughed.

Greta's smile didn't reach her eyes. She squeezed Alana's hand over the table. "I'm so happy for you, honey. Really. You deserve this."

"Like I said, it isn't for sure yet."

"But you went after it anyway," Greta offered.

A waiter arrived to take their order. Greta ordered a white wine while Alana ordered a rose. They were seated outside beneath an umbrella that blocked the generous sunrays on this side of the street. Just down the street, you can see the green froth of hundreds of Central Park trees.

"It's a beautiful day," Alana offered because silence was heavy on the table.

"Yes."

Alana pressed her lips together. "You don't have to talk about it if you don't want to."

The waiter returned with their wines, and Greta thanked him too many times as though she wanted to stall. Finally, she raised her glass and said, "I don't know what to make of any of it. I feel like I don't live on a planet I understand."

"Welcome to the club."

Greta laughed and pressed the back of her wrist to her forehead.

"Come on. What did he say?" Alana pressed it.

"He didn't even know she wrote fiction," Greta rasped, still staring at the table between them. "He said the most creative he ever saw her was writing advertisement copy or fingerpainting with their kids. It's like she wanted to turn her back completely on her old life. Like she no longer cared about music or books or art. Everything that the two of us shared during that year together."

Alana's heart panged with sorrow. "That's so strange."

"But it gets weirder. Apparently, Celeste didn't tell her husband that she had met me in Nantucket. He didn't even know about me at all."

"It sounds like she really wanted to see you. But she didn't want to reveal these parts of herself to him," Alana went on. "I guess I can understand that. Sort of."

Alana thought again about how she still hadn't told Jeremy about her audition, and her stomach twisted.

Greta banged her fist on the table. "Then why didn't she say anything to me? Why didn't she tell me what was really on her mind? Why did she talk to me about the weather when her life was on the brink of ending?" Greta's face squeezed into a red ball, and she burst into tears.

Alana was on her feet. She'd never seen her mother so emotional before, and it sent her own emotions into a downward spiral. She threw her arms around Greta from the side and said anything she could to calm her down.

"She loved you so much, Mom. Sometimes, we don't know how to share our love with each other. But it's clear she needed to see you before she died. You were like a mother to her for so long. You were like a mother when she really needed a mother."

But this only seemed to stress Greta out more. She pressed a linen napkin over her face and shuddered and sobbed. Eventually, Alana alerted the waiter that she would pay for the wine and take her mother out. The waiter seemed relieved. Greta was scaring the other diners, all of whom were looking at her and gossiping into one another's ears. Their whispers were like lizards in the grass.

Alana hailed a taxi and took Greta back to the hotel they'd both booked for the night. In the back of the car, Greta pressed her hand over her mouth and hiccupped a few times, but she didn't keep crying. The driver kept trying to talk to Alana about how beautiful the weather was and where she was from, but Alana answered so curtly that he eventually got the hint.

Alana led Greta to her hotel room and poured her a big glass of water with ice. Greta sat at the edge of Alana's bed and muttered, "I'm so sorry. I can't believe I lost control like that."

"We all lose control sometimes," Alana said. "It's part of being alive."

Alana sat quietly with her mother for over a half-hour before Greta perked up a bit. By then, Sarah texted that she was getting out of rehearsal early; would they like to go out to eat? Alana texted that they wanted to stay in, but she would buy everyone room service if Sarah wanted to come by. Sarah leaped at the chance. "Room service is the best!" she texted.

Greta splayed across Alana's bed and stretched her arms out on either side. "I want a cheeseburger and extra fries," she said.

"That sounds delicious," Alana said after a brief pause. It was rare her mother went for such American greasy fare. "I'll have the same."

Not long after that, Sarah arrived, and Alana called for room service. Sarah was peppy after all day of rehearsing, and she engaged Greta in easy small talk about all things off-Broadway until Greta's smiles became easy rather than forced.

"You have to teach me this dance," Greta urged Sarah, and Sarah popped up and taught Greta all the moves to the dance Sarah's character performed in Act II. Greta followed along and laughed until she urged Alana to pop up and try it, too.

"I feel like I have three feet and eight arms," Alana said as she messed up the dance for the fifth time. "Mom, how have you already gotten this down?"

"She's a natural," Sarah said.

"You're just a good teacher," Greta assured her. She winked at Alana knowingly.

It felt as though Alana and Greta had just shared the most intimate afternoon of their lives. Greta was the only person in the world (besides Pete and his employees) who knew Alana had auditioned for a play today, and Alana was the only person in the world who understood a smidgeon of the devastation Greta was going through in the wake of losing Celeste—a woman she couldn't possibly comprehend. As Alana, Greta, and Sarah tore through their burgers that evening and watched reality television, Alana felt as though she floated a few inches off the bed. This was her family. This was her life. And she was doing what she could to make herself and those around her as happy as she could. It occurred to her that Celeste had lived the same way, that pursuing art just hadn't offered the same rewards any longer. And in a world where so little ever made sense, maybe that was okay.

# Chapter Fifteen

Greta woke up in Alana's hotel room and in Alana's bed. She felt a strange wave of comfort at the memory of the last time she and Alana had shared a bed. It must have been more than forty years ago when Alana had suffered from nightmares. It must have been the time before Alana knew how to show her anger to Greta and before Greta grew to resent Alana. How Greta wished she could take that back!

Alana had tended to Greta yesterday with the sort of mastery, empathy, and love of a mother. She'd intuitively known Greta's needs and gotten her out of the restaurant. And she'd let her hole up in her hotel room and hide herself away from the ache of her own emotions.

But now it was time for Greta to go back home.

Greta got up, made a cup of coffee, and drank it quietly. Alana still didn't stir when she got into the shower, dressed and packed her little bag. It was only when Greta touched her shoulder that Alana erupted with a start and said, "What time is it? Did I miss it?"

Alana blinked and then collapsed back on the pillow. "Sorry. I had a dream that I missed my audition."

"That was yesterday," Greta said with a laugh. "But I know those kinds of dreams well."

Alana sat up in bed, and Greta pressed a cup of fresh coffee into her hands. "It's ten minutes after nine," she said. "I'm going to check out of my room and head back to Nantucket. I don't like leaving your father alone too long."

Greta knew this was because so much time had been taken away from them. She wanted to spend every moment she could with him—even the dull moments, the in-between moments. She wanted to yawn beside him, laugh with him and watch bad television. She wanted to make stovetop popcorn and escape the sorrow of what she'd learned.

She hugged Alana. "I love you, sweetheart. Thank you for everything."

"I love you, too."

"When are you meeting the director to talk about the play?"

"Friday," Alana said resignedly. "I know it'll be tricky with Fourth of July and everything."

"You'll make it work. When are you heading home?"

"Probably tomorrow morning," Alana said.

"You're getting pretty used to that drive."

"I hope to get really used to it," Alana offered. "I hope to make it a part of my lifestyle."

Greta touched her daughter's hair and prayed beyond anything that Alana would get what she wanted. Her eyes were filled with light.

* * *

Greta got home a little after three that afternoon to find Bernard asleep on the back porch. He had his shirt off and a pair of jeans on, and he'd folded his hands over his chest and tipped his head back. His breath was light and sweet. Greta tried to tip-toe off the porch and back to the kitchen, but the screen door screamed and woke him up.

"Hello?" He looked flustered.

"It's me," Greta said sweetly. She returned to him and pressed a kiss on his lips.

"My girl's in from the big city. How did it go?"

Greta grimaced. "Lots to say. But it's so good to see you."

Bernard stood up, and his body creaked and popped. "Look at me? I'm falling apart without you here."

Greta laughed and wrapped her arms around him. "You look perfect to me."

Bernard suggested they go on a walk before dinner so that he could wake up a little and stretch his legs. He buttoned up his shirt and talked about the past couple of days, how James had come over with a few of his friends, and Bernard had made them frozen pizzas that had turned out "like poison, or worse. I don't know how I messed them up so badly. James was begging me to call you back home."

Greta laughed and laced her arm through Bernard's as they stepped out onto the sand. A wind kicked up from the Sound and spit bits of sand over their ankles. They were quiet for a good five minutes before Bernard said, "Are you going to tell me what happened? Or do you want to keep it for yourself?"

Greta sighed. She knew she owed Bernard an explanation. She wasn't in the habit of keeping things from him during this era of their marriage. There was no point to it.

So briefly, she explained what she'd learned about Celeste from her husband. It was a miracle she didn't burst into tears this time.

"You should have seen me at this restaurant," Greta said. "I was a mess. And I couldn't explain to Alana exactly what was wrong. It took me an entire drive back to Nantucket to fully grasp it."

Bernard furrowed his brow. He wanted her to go on.

"Around a year after she arrived, Celeste started talking about moving to New York to pursue play-wrighting and possibly directing. I was over the moon. She had so much talent. So much skill. And she'd already teased me, saying, 'Who says I'll ever leave Nantucket?' I'd given her speech after speech about how I was washed up, and she was the one with the future career. So, this was proof that my speeches had actually worked. We set to work perfecting the script we'd written together, and we got it into a really good place right before she left."

"I'm sure it was a masterpiece," Bernard interjected.

"The night before she left, I cooked an enormous meal," Greta went on. "And we toasted her future career and future success. But all at once, she burst into tears and hugged me and begged me to let her stay. I'd never seen her like that before. It scared me. In retrospect, there was so much she wasn't telling me about her past. She'd never told me about some stranger she'd been with before Nantucket, someone who'd probably hurt her. And she'd never told me about her mother and father and how lonely it had been growing up there. I couldn't have known that I was this mother figure for her. Although..." Greta trailed off and wrung her hands. "Although I should have known! Part of me did know! But instead, I took her hands and said, 'You've come too far to give up on yourself.' And I remember what she said so clearly. It's been echoing in my head ever since I found out she died. She said, 'I want to stay here. I want to build a life here. I don't care about that other stuff.' Of course, this mortified me. I said, 'What do you mean you don't care? That's what life is all about! It's about art and music and pushing yourself! If you don't go, you'll regret it forever.' And I was the only person in her life. I was closing the door in her face. She basically had to go."

Greta's lips trembled at the memory, and she pressed her face against Bernard's chest. They stopped walking so that he could hold her as the Nantucket wind tore at their clothes.

"It wasn't your fault, Greta," Bernard said. "You didn't cause any of that other stuff to happen. You saw potential, and you wanted to hone it. It's what we'd been doing at The Copperfield House for years!"

"But I knew how much pain she was in," Greta offered. "I should have done something about it. Maybe I should have moved to New York City and helped her along. I shouldn't have made her go into the world alone." She bit her lip. "Maybe she wouldn't have gone through so much turmoil."

Bernard took her small hands in his and locked eyes with her.

"I pushed her out, and I pushed her into a life that ultimately ended in misery. She gave up on her dreams anyway, maybe because being loved and protected was always more important to her. I didn't offer her enough of that," Greta went on. She was speaking too quickly. She couldn't keep track of what she'd already said. It was all pouring out.

"You gave her all the love you had," Bernard said tenderly.

"It wasn't enough," Greta said.

Bernard tugged her back into him and held her for a long time. Greta listened to the steady beat of his heart and felt herself dissolve. All she could think about were those four little kids who no longer had their mother, along with the devastating fact that they would never know the version of Celeste that Greta had known. They would never know the magic of her writing nor of her heart. And wasn't that a tragedy?

# Chapter Sixteen

It was Alana's final day in New York City before her planned return tomorrow. Sarah was going out with a few members of the cast. Ginny had a date, so she was on her own. But she didn't mind. Her thoughts were moving so quickly that she wanted to walk the streets and live in her head and make sense of this brand-new opportunity alongside her brand-new marriage—both things she loved so much that her heart grew too big for her ribcage. But toward the end of the night, Ginny texted:

> "We're going out tomorrow! I want to celebrate something!"

Alana laughed. She was already in bed at the hotel, waiting for sleep. "I was supposed to leave tomorrow!"

> GINNY: You have to postpone. Seriously. I need my number one girl!

> ALANA: What are we celebrating?

GINNY: I'll tell you tomorrow. But you
HAVE to stay. Just one more night.
Please?

Alana sighed and called Jeremy. He picked up after two rings. "Good evening, my lady," he said in a fake English accent.

Alana giggled and rolled over onto her stomach. She felt like a teenager when she spoke to him sometimes, as it ripped her right back into the early nineties. She wiggled her toes. "Whatcha up to?"

"I'm watching television, of course," Jeremy said. "I just have one more night of watching whatever I want before my ball and chain comes back to hog the screen."

"You better not be watching anything I want to watch," Alana said.

"I would never."

Alana smiled so big into the phone that her cheeks nearly cracked. *Tell him about the audition. Tell him about the play.* But instead, she heard herself say, "Listen, Ginny invited me out tomorrow night. She wants to celebrate something."

"Ah! The television is mine for one more night."

Alana giggled. "You don't mind?"

"I don't mind. As long as you promise to come back eventually," Jeremy said. "I don't want to have that wedding all by myself. Although I wouldn't mind eating all that cake myself."

"It's tricky. When you get married, you legally have to share everything," Alana teased.

"I know. It's tough," Jeremy joked.

Alana's heart pounded. It would be so simple to explain everything to him, to translate just how much it meant to her to get back into acting, to echo the ache of her jealousy for Sarah and Ginny's lives. But at the same time, all she could do was picture Jeremy on the sofa at home with a big bowl of popcorn on his lap. She could see herself curled up alongside him with her head on his shoulder. She could hear them bickering into infinity about what to watch now and what to watch later until one of them inevitably fell asleep early. She loved that life! She loved the life they'd built together! She felt squeezed.

"I love you and miss you," Alana said instead.

"Right back at you. Give my daughter a big hug when you see her," Jeremy said.

"I always do."

"And you're coming back Wednesday. Right?"

"Yes." Alana didn't mention that she was headed back to the city on Friday because she still couldn't visualize. She couldn't imagine ripping herself from her family obligations—from hot dogs and s'mores and her mother's laughter and fireworks—to go hang out with Pete in some dark Manhattan bar. *It's for your career,* she reminded herself. But it still just didn't quite fit her. Like a sweater, she was trying to force on she'd outgrown long ago.

Right after she got off the phone with Jeremy, Pete texted her. It was almost as if he sensed her doubts.

PETE: Still can't get over your audition.

PETE: You're going places, kid.

Alana grimaced and then pushed herself to text back.

ALANA: I'm not a kid anymore. Ha.

PETE: That's for the better. Don't you think there's too much young blood in the theater world? Don't we want to see real people and real actors up on that stage?

Pete's words slipped into her bloodstream like fine wine and emboldened her. She fell asleep half-dreaming about her future and woke up with a smile on her face. Ginny wrote to say how excited she was for tonight, and Sarah wrote to say she was coming out, too. A few others from the play were joining. Alana felt everything coming together. She felt as though she was a part of the squad.

Ginny booked them at a table at a nearly impossible-to-get-into bar, as usual. It was in Harlem, of all places—a swanky speakeasy with tables located behind a door that required a specific type of knock to open. Alana had seen things like this all over the world, including Paris, Bangkok, and Beijing, but it had been a while, and it filled her with wonder. When they sat, Ginny ordered them the most exclusive cocktail on the menu—made with elder-flower and coconut cream—and placed her hands together as she said, "The minute we have our drinks, I'll make my announcement."

Sarah laughed and turned toward her three friends from the play. They were all slightly older than Sarah, and it was clear to Alana that they were showing her the "rules" of being in the theater world. Sarah cracked jokes with them and spoke in a way that surprised Alana. Just a month ago, Sarah had called Alana, sobbing and begging for her to come to Manhattan to save her. That had faded.

Alana wondered if this was what it felt like to watch a real child grow up. Parents always talked about the loss when they stopped needing to hold your hand to cross the street or stopped asking to sleep in your bed.

"Tell me about your lives," Alana asked Sarah's friends, which may have been a mistake. They were theater people, and they loved to talk about themselves.

The one sitting directly next to Sarah had bright red hair and an angry look to her. "I'm a born-and-bred New Yorker," she said. "I went to Columbia to get a political justice degree. See how well that worked out."

Sarah sputtered with laughter. "You minored in acting, right?"

"No. I minored in business to make my dad happy," the redhead said with a snort. "I auditioned for a play a few years ago without telling anyone and ended up getting a larger part than I'd auditioned for."

"How did your dad react?" Alana asked.

"He freaked," the redhead admitted. "I didn't think he was going to come to the play, especially after I quit my job. But he ended up coming on the very last night. I didn't know he was there till after when he approached with a bouquet. It was literally like something out of a movie. He told me he was proud of me. That he always knew I was going to become something."

"Aww," everyone at the table cooed in unison.

The redhead waved her hands. "Yeah, yeah. But it comes with wave after wave of heartache. Obviously, this business isn't for people who can't take it." She locked eyes with Alana and added, "I know you know that better than most. Right? Sarah showed me your advertisements."

Alana felt a pang in her gut. She had to bite her tongue to keep herself from saying, *Well, your director is about to cast me in a play. I'm practically already in the play. I'm already in.*

The cocktails arrived, and Ginny clapped her hands and said it was time to announce something major. "Everyone, take your cocktails and raise them up," she instructed, and everyone did what she said. Music hummed in the background and buzzed through Alana's limbs. Ginny looked gorgeous in the candlelight. She looked gorgeous all the time. *What would it be like to have that life? What would it be like to still have it all?*

"Pete has booked me for his next play!" Ginny cried.

"Oh my gosh!" This came from the redhead, who set down her cocktail and reached over to take Ginny's hand. "You didn't even have to audition, did you? He loves you so much."

Ginny laughed and closed her eyes so tightly that her skin wrinkled. "I can't believe I'm still getting roles this late in life. I genuinely feel so grateful." She opened her eyes again to lock them with Alana and added, "And I just love so much that my old friend is here with me. We've taken dramatically different paths in life, but I still feel like we get each other. Don't you, A?"

Alana's throat was tight. Because she was still a good actress, she could act her way out of a paper bag; she maintained a smile. But her heart banged. "Congratulations, honey! What part did you get?" she asked. "Tell us more!"

*Don't say Martha. Don't say Martha.* Oh gosh. If Ginny was going to play Martha, Alana would probably throw up across the table.

"I'm playing Henrietta," Ginny said. "She has a crazy backstory that plays out over the course of the play. It's going to take a lot of character work, I think."

"Are you going to go method actor on us?" Another of Sarah's friends asked.

Ginny giggled. "Maybe! I don't have a boyfriend or any kids or anything. I can act however I want to, and nobody will be the wiser. Maybe I'll meet a whole different group of friends."

That's when Alana noticed Sarah's smile. It was secretive and gorgeous, and the tops of her cheeks glowed red. After coaching Sarah in acting for two years, Alana had grown accustomed to seeing the "real" Sarah come to the surface. This was the real Sarah.

"What are you hiding?" Alana asked, teasing her. Now that Ginny wasn't playing Martha, she could breathe easier.

"Um?" Sarah laughed as the others at the table urged her to say.

"I can see it written all over your face," the redhead said. "Come on. You have something. A secret. And there are no secrets between friends! Not in theater. That's where gossip sings."

Alana smiled wider as Sarah made a big show of "allowing" herself to share. She took a deep breath and said, "Okay. Okay. Pete cast me in his play, too."

Ginny shrieked and erupted from the table to wrap Sarah in a hug. The others cried out, although Alana hinted at flickers of jealousy passing over each of the actresses' faces. The ones who hadn't yet been chosen.

"I can't believe neither of you had to audition," the redhead said. Alana made a mental note to ask her name, but maybe it was too awkward now.

"Pete loves you guys," Sarah assured them. "I'm sure he has you in mind for the other parts."

"We'll see," the redhead said.

"Which part are you playing?" Ginny asked.

"I'm Martha," Sarah said.

Alana had just taken a sip of cocktail. It immediately went down the wrong tube. She huffed and whacked her chest as she coughed. Everyone at the table and across the speakeasy turned to gawk at her. She sounded like a dying chicken.

"Are you okay?" Sarah popped up to fetch her some water from a nearby cooler. "Drink this."

Alana's smile was practically manic. "I'm fine! Really. I'm sorry. I'm just so happy for you both. It's going to be another incredible play. And it's always amazing to have your next project booked before the first one ends!" She remembered this well from her modeling days.

Alana sipped her water as the others continued to banter about Sarah and Ginny's good luck. Alana's heart felt heavy as stone. She felt as though she could sink off the chair and fall to the floor, and never get up again. But each time somebody at the table addressed her, she was able to perk up and answer their question. She was able to pretend to be thrilled.

And really, she told herself, she WAS thrilled. Sarah was her soon-to-be stepdaughter. She was only nineteen and already a sought-after actress in the off-Broadway circuit. Pete and directors like Pete were apt to fight over her in the future. Her career was flung out before her like a red carpet.

Alana excused herself to the bathroom and checked her phone in the stall. She was beginning to doubt that she'd auditioned at all, and she had to check to see if Pete had actually been texting her all day. In fact, he'd written her twelve times just that afternoon. Every single one referred to Alana's future career—both in his play and in other plays. Every single one built a future that Pete didn't actually believe in.

He'd wound her up. But why?

Alana felt sick. She felt old and used up and, above all, sad. She left the stall and sat in a luxurious chair in the bathroom to gaze at herself in the mirror. This woman was in her late forties. She thought for sure she was about to take on an off-Broadway role that had ultimately gone to a nineteen-year-old. Who was she kidding?

Alana felt the edges of her life crinkling up. She felt her world coming to an end. And she told herself it was okay; it was really okay. She had Jeremy. She had the love of her life. But this didn't stop tears from draining from her eyes and rolling to her chin.

But more than anything, she knew that Pete had created this situation out of his own sick will. This meant he was capable of even darker situations, of destroying people's will.

Beyond anything, Alana had to protect Sarah. She had to hang around Manhattan just a smidgen longer to warn him that she was on to him. And she had very little patience when it came to guys like him. She'd been married to one—and she refused to let anyone else play her like that again.

* * *

Alana kept up the ruse of her own happiness all night long. At some point, Ginny ordered them shots; at another, Sarah and the redhead (whose name was Bobbi) dragged them off to karaoke and dancing. Alana eventually felt herself fully ooze into the night. She wrapped her arms around Sarah on the dance floor and cried, "Your dad and I are so proud of you!" And Sarah wrinkled her nose and said, "That's so cringy, Alana!" "It's Mom," Alana joked back as Sarah cackled. Obviously, she would never call Alana that. But their humor was in sync—which was more important.

The next morning, Alana woke up with a headache and a resolution about not having any more nights out in Manhattan like that. Not now. She was too old for it. She'd moved on. She now ached to throw herself back to Nantucket, wrap her arms around Jeremy and argue about what was on television. It was now her only potential future.

But she still knew she had to tell him about all of this. This fact sunk into her belly like too much bread.

Alana showered, did her makeup and checked the time. The play rehearsal was set for nine-thirty that morning with a lunch break at once. Alana planned to be there for all of it. After that, she would say goodbye to Sarah, leap into her car, and drive home. Her fingers burned to start the engine and speed home.

Alana slipped into rehearsal a few minutes before. Pete was in conversation with three actors in the production, saying things so arrogant that they burned Alana's ears. She said a silent prayer that she wouldn't be working with that man, then another that involved protecting Sarah. By the time all the players were on the stage, Alana's blood pressure had spiked, and she couldn't look away—not even when Sarah was backstage and awaiting her next appearance. Alana allowed herself to get lost in the magic of this production as they worked out all the kinks and found their way.

Pete called lunch ten minutes late, and the actors fled the stage to grab their sandwiches in back and crack jokes.

Pete remained at his table as he always did, scratching his forehead as he read over notes he'd made during rehearsal. Alana approached, silent as a deer in the forest. When she reached the table, her heart was beating so quickly that she thought she might faint. But she had to do what she'd come to do.

"Hello, Peter."

Pete flinched and turned toward her. He smiled arrogantly and handsomely. "There's my girl."

"Cut the crap," Alana shot.

Pete raised his eyebrows and laughed. "Beg your pardon?"

"You know what I'm talking about."

Pete laughed again. "I hope you bring this energy to dinner on Friday. I love a woman who tells me how wrong I am."

Alana felt flames come out of her ears. "I'm not coming to dinner with you on Friday."

"Okay. What about Saturday?" His eyes sparkled with intrigue. He clearly loved a challenge.

"Listen. I don't care what you do to me," Alana shot. "You can make fun of me. You can belittle my career. Whatever." She pointed backstage. "But I want you to know I'm watching you. If you ever do anything to hurt the career of that young woman back there, if you ever mess with her emotions or her pride or her sense of herself, I will come after you. I will do all I can to destroy you. Remember that I still know people in this industry."

Pete's eyes flickered with a mix of curiosity and rage. But after a pregnant pause, he bowed his head and said, "I hear you loud and clear, Alana Copperfield."

Alana unclenched her fists. She hadn't realized how hard she'd been squeezing. "Okay. Okay, thank you." She let out a breath and took a step back. The further she got away from him, the better she felt.

"I really do think you're talented," Pete said. "Or, I did. Back when you had that special something."

"Back when I was young, you mean."

Pete's laugh was sinister. "That's showbiz, baby." He then returned his gaze to his script and made a note as though Alana hadn't been there at all.

But Pete couldn't take away the fact that Alana had stood up to him. She'd said her piece and demanded something of him, and now she was free to take off for her car and drive the five hours back to Hyannis Port. She wasn't needed back in Manhattan for weeks—not till opening night. And as she cranked the engine and opened the windows, her heart began to sing with relief.

# Chapter Seventeen

Greta's agent, Cynthia, called her on the morning of the Fourth of July. "I'm sorry to bother you like this," Cynthia began without saying hello, "but I just received an exciting email, and I wanted to let you know about it right away."

Greta was in her robe in the kitchen of The Copperfield House with a mug of coffee. Out along the beach were Catherine and Quentin, walking hand-in-hand as the water burst up along the sands. Catherine's hair whipped out around her, newly grown and vibrant after her battle with cancer. Greta's heart swelled. She knew they were on their way here for a Fourth of July breakfast followed by a barbecue and non-stop action till the exhilarating finish once night fell. And that was just the beginning. Fourth of July fell on a Thursday this year, which meant that the island would ramp up for an entire weekend of festivities. Greta couldn't wait.

"Are you there, Greta?" Cynthia asked.

"Sorry. I'm not quite awake yet," Greta offered with a laugh. "What's up?"

"I chatted to someone in Hollywood about your new manuscript," Cynthia said. "There's a possibility that they want to option it and make it into a film."

Greta narrowed her eyes with shock. Rather than leap up and down with excitement, her heart slowed. "My manuscript? You mean the one I've hardly started? The one about Celeste?"

"Yes. Like I told you already, there's a huge market interested in your life while you lived in The Copperfield House alone," Cynthia went on. "You know how it is. Some people think you got up to your own mischief in there. I read rumors online that suggested you were practicing witchcraft!"

Greta snorted and filled her mouth with coffee. What would people think of next?

"I'm only just getting a handle on the story itself," Greta said finally. "I can't fathom how this could be a movie. It's going to be extremely poetic and introspective."

"Greta, are you trying to kill me?"

Greta snorted with surprised laughter. "I'm sorry?"

"These people want to throw money at you! At us! And you want to turn them away?"

"There are more important things than money," Greta offered with a soft smile. "My story and Celeste's story are priceless. And I don't want to change them on the surface of some faceless production studio. Do you?"

Cynthia grumbled. "I don't know?"

Greta rolled her eyes and laughed again.

"If you were younger, you would say yes," Cynthia offered. "You would say it in a heartbeat."

"You can always replace me with a younger client, you know," Greta said.

Cynthia sighed. "But I actually love you, Greta. You know I'm your number one fan."

"I appreciate that. I do. But I also can't accept this. I'm sorry." Greta set down her mug as Quentin and Catherine entered the front door without knocking. "I have to run. Happy Fourth of July, Cynthia. Put this out of your mind. It just isn't happening, okay?"

"Fine," Cynthia groaned. "Love you."

"Love you back."

Greta swarmed Catherina and Quentin, hugging them and asking how their walk was filled with mugs of coffee and pressing them into their hands.

"We're early!" Catherine said when she saw what Greta was wearing.

"You're not. I got a slow start to the day," Greta said. She wouldn't share the reason for it; she wouldn't tell her adult son and his adult wife that she and her husband Bernard had spent the morning in bed together. But she hoped that when Quentin and Catherine were older, they wouldn't give up on each other the way some couples did. She hoped they found love in all its forms down the line.

Greta hurried upstairs to find Bernard coming out of the shower and toweling his wild gray and black hair. She kissed him and said, "Quentin and Catherine are already here!" as Bernard stepped into a pair of boxers and snapped them at his waist. "I have to start on breakfast," Greta went on as she hurriedly dressed in a red dress and pulled her hair tie out of her long and lustrous hair. Bernard came up behind her and kissed her shoulder, making eye contact with her in the mirror. Something stirred in Greta's chest, and she considered falling back in bed with him and avoiding the world. But it was the

Fourth of July—and their entire family was coming over! It was a dream.

"Cynthia just called," Greta informed him evenly as she put on makeup. "She says they want to make my book a film."

Bernard snorted. "The one that isn't written yet?"

"The very one. I told her it wasn't for sale. It's one thing to have total control over Celeste and my story on the page; it's another to hand it over to a television studio."

"Thatta girl."

Downstairs, several more Copperfields had gathered. Scarlet and Ivy carried two trays of cheddar biscuits that they'd baked at home, and Ella and Will were stationed at the kitchen table with big mugs of coffee. Danny and Laura put Bruce Springsteen's "Born in the USA" on the record player and clapped to get everyone excited for the day ahead. Greta breezed past them and kissed them as she made her way to the stove to make heaps of eggs and bacon. As she worked more and more, Copperfield's arrived, and Danny and Laura repeated "Born in the USA" endlessly until Quentin ordered them in an authoritative voice to play "anything else in the world." When they changed it to "Come on, Eileen," Quentin cried with pain and went onto the porch. Everyone in the kitchen cackled.

"He's always hated that song," Alana said as she carried a big plate of crispy bacon from the kitchen to the back porch table. "I used to torment him with it in high school."

"Yeah, how did you know that?" Ella called to her children in the next room. "How did you know Uncle Quentin hated that song so much?"

"Lucky guess!" Laura called back.

"Everyone hates that song!" Danny said.

"I don't," Julia said as she crunched a carrot and looked out the window. "I always listen to it when I need to pep myself up between writing and editing sessions."

Alana returned and giggled. "I can just picture you in your office, listening to 'Come on, Eileen' on repeat with big, manic eyes."

Julia swatted her and smiled. Greta watched her three daughters from her typical stance at the stovetop and felt a wave of emotion choke her up. It occurred to her that she had maybe ten or fifteen years left of this sort of gorgeous dynamic. Maybe twenty, if she was lucky. There was no telling how many years anybody had left. You had to put yourself at the mercy of time.

Alana leaned against the counter and held her coffee mug with both hands. Greta remembered how tenderly Alana had cared for her in New York. Without her, she wouldn't have gotten through that day. Her heart still felt cracked at the edges. But it would heal. It had to.

Greta wondered if Alana had told Jeremy anything about her audition yet. She wondered if Alana would share how that had gone or if she would keep it to herself to protect her relationship. Greta respected both options.

And then, Alana offered up the situation on a platter for her sisters. "I auditioned for an off-Broadway play this week."

Ella's jaw dropped. "What! You didn't!"

Julia swatted her on the shoulder. "How did it go?"

"Horribly," Alana said. Her eyes glinted with embarrassment. Greta wished she could wipe it away. "The director basically told me I got the part and then ripped it out from under me. I'm pretty sure he was trying to date me in a roundabout way by manipulating me. Or maybe he just wanted control. I don't know."

Ella's mouth hung open wider. "That's so typical of the music business. I was always with Will, but people were always trying to do that to me. Manipulate me. Tell me that my career would be so much better if I just went back to their hotel room with them. Disgusting."

"It takes such a strong stomach to be in the music and acting businesses," Julia offered.

Alana sighed and made eye contact with Greta. Greta offered her kindest smile.

"I've been trying to get up the energy to explain to Jeremy what happened," Alana said.

"What do you mean?" Ella asked.

"I didn't tell him about the audition in the first place," Alana said. "It feels like a betrayal."

"But you didn't know that guy was going to be such a dirtbag," Julia said.

Alana raised her shoulders. "True. But I got carried away with my own dreams. And I didn't include Jeremy in them. It's like high school all over again. And we're just a few weeks from the wedding!"

"He'll understand," Ella assured her with a wave of her hand. "Jeremy loves you no matter what."

Alana's chin quivered. "I hope you're right."

Suddenly, Sarah bounded into the kitchen with Jeremy hot on her heels. Greta hadn't known Sarah was joining them. "You got out of rehearsals?" Greta cried as she collected the girl in a hug.

"We don't have any all weekend," Sarah said. Her hug was extra tight. It felt as though the city had made her stronger.

Greta still ached with the memory of when Sarah had

been skin and bones. She watched as Alana kissed Jeremy with her eyes closed and asked, "How was your night in the city?"

"I don't think we got up to as much as you guys normally do," Jeremy said with a laugh. "But Sarah showed me her favorite burger place, and I have to admit it's almost as good as our place here in Nantucket. Almost."

"Come on! It's way better," Sarah said.

"No. Just almost better," Jeremy teased.

That Fourth of July was one for the ages. Every single Copperfield and close Copperfield relative came over to eat breakfast, walk along the beach, and fly kites in the sterling blue sky above. By noon, the barbecue was smoking, and by one-thirty, everyone was eating hot dogs and hamburgers and inhaling chips and pretzels and Cheez-Its. Greta made margaritas for herself and the girls, and the boys stuck to beer and swapped funny stories and laughed. Eventually, everyone put on swimsuits and ran out into the Nantucket Sound. Their bodies were glistening beneath the sun.

For dinner, they feasted on barbecue chicken and grilled vegetables, then made s'mores around the bonfire as the light died overhead. A smattering of stars came next, followed by explosion after explosion of an iconic array of fireworks. They came from near the lighthouse and a few larger ships offshore. It was like the light was coming from all directions. Greta placed her head on Bernard's chest and listened to her family "ohh" and "aww" over the display. Jeremy and Alana were cozied up together on a blanket on the beach with their arms around one another. Sarah was over with the other teenagers and twenty-somethings, all of whom had probably eaten them out of house and home today and planned to go back for thirds when the fireworks were through.

For whatever reason, Greta thought back to the Fourth of Julys that she and Celeste had spent together. They'd sat out on the back porch with glasses of white wine and remained quiet as the fireworks exploded overhead. It often felt as though they were the only two people in the world, as though it was just them on a rock floating through outer space. But the truth was there were billions of people out there. And the fireworks were proof of that. It was difficult to know if they would join them one day or if they would remain at The Copperfield House forever.

# Chapter Eighteen

Sarah explained breezily that she wanted to stay at Scarlet and Ivy's that night instead of home with Alana and Jeremy. Alana felt it like a needle through her heart. For whatever reason, she wanted Jeremy, Sarah, and herself to sleep all in one house that night. She wanted to feel like a family. But Jeremy said, "Of course! Have a great time," and hugged his daughter goodnight like the wonderful father he was. Alana couldn't have loved him more.

Alana and Jeremy walked back to their place that night as still more fireworks lit up the night sky. She wasn't sure the island would ever run out of them. She squeezed Jeremy's hand a little too tight as they went, and he hissed and said, "Ouch!" then laughed. "Sorry. You have a football player's grip!"

Alana laughed and tossed her head back. Her heart felt bruised. "I have to tell you something, Jeremy."

Jeremy stopped walking and looked at her like an injured deer. He looked terrified that she was about to do something drastic, like get an entirely new face with plastic surgery or, try to make it as an online gambler, or just break up with him. Probably it was the last one. His hand literally shook.

"It's nothing that bad," Alana said softly.

Jeremy's shoulders loosened just the slightest bit, but he didn't smile. "Just tell me. I can handle it."

Alana swallowed the lump in her throat. "Recently, Sarah's director asked me to audition for his next play. And I said yes."

Jeremy's eyes widened, but he remained quiet. Waiting.

"I didn't know what to make of it. It freaked me out how much I suddenly wanted that life again. I decided to just go for it and see where the chips fell," Alana went on. "In retrospect, I should have called you the minute he asked me to audition. But I was scared you would see it as me turning my back on you. We've already been through that in our lives before. And I definitely didn't want to do that to you again. I genuinely love you, Jeremy. I love you with everything I am. And I can't wait to marry you at the end of the month. But I couldn't ignore this huge desire to make it. I had these two things in my head at once."

Jeremy's eyes were light again. Probably because Alana continued to tell him how much she loved him and wanted to still marry him. He recognized that whatever happened, Alana would still walk down the aisle.

"You got the part, didn't you?" Jeremy asked, palming the back of his neck.

Alana's chest caved in. Tears sprung to her eyes. "I didn't." She sniffed. "But it's worse than that. I think the director was trying to manipulate me. It felt just like old times with Asher. And it totally destroyed my confidence.

I haven't been able to tell you because it's all so embarrassing. That, and I don't want you to think I don't love you."

Alana burst into tears, and Jeremy collected her in his arms and swayed with her as the fireworks blasted overhead. Alana could feel the steady beat of his heart through her entire body. She felt cocooned.

"I would be lying if I said I wasn't hurt," Jeremy offered quietly.

Alana felt her heart crack at the edges. "I know. I knew you would be."

Jeremy kissed the top of her head and pulled her tighter against him. He sighed. "I know what it's like to want something so badly. I know that it's consuming."

Alana sensed that he was talking about Notre Dame again, about a football career that seemed laid out for him, about a future that should have been his if it weren't for that horrendous car accident and a night that had altered both of their lives forever.

"I don't think I ever told you that I went there," Jeremy said as he continued to hold her. "I drove all the way out to Notre Dame during that first season. You were already in the city with Asher, and my life was nothing. I was so depressed. Dead inside. I thought maybe a long drive would shake my sorrows out of me. I thought maybe going to Notre Dame would free me of something that was weighing me down. But when I got there, it was twenty-two degrees, and it was snowing. I sat way back in the stands, shivering as I watched the team that should have been my team lose by twenty-three points. I stayed through every minute, maybe as a way to punish myself."

Alana could feel his sad smile. It was her turn to hold him tighter. "I'm so sorry, baby. I'm so sorry."

"It's okay. It was an important lesson for me," Jeremy

said. "I learned to put the past behind me that day. I still remember staying in a hotel in that little rinky-dink university town and flicking through the stations to watch reruns of Seinfeld. I knew you were off having this glamorous life, and I wasn't sure if anything would ever happen for me. But I sat there and laughed myself to sleep. And in the morning, there was so much light spilling through the hotel's windows. I'll never forget that."

Alana and Jeremy continued to hold each other for a long time before they released their hug and walked hand-in-hand back home. There was an air of empathy, of understanding. When they reached the front porch, Alana squeezed his hand a final time and said, "I'm going to make sure Sarah is okay in this world. Nobody can mess with her."

But Jeremy just said, "I think Sarah can already take care of herself," with a smile. And Alana knew that he was right.

# Chapter Nineteen

The weekend before Alana and Jeremy's wedding was Sarah's first performance in Manhattan. Alana and Jeremy drove down that morning, holding hands between the seats as they raced toward that glinting horizon where their girl was making her way toward stardom. Greta, Bernard, Julia, Ella, and Will were coming in separate cars; Scarlet was already in the city with her mother, Quentin, James, and Ivy, and Laura was going to stop by to see it later that week on her way to Nantucket for the wedding. It was clear that everyone in the Copperfield family took her artistry seriously; they wanted to make time for her. They wanted to let her know she was loved.

Jeremy and Alana parked right in front of Sarah's apartment in the Lower East Side. "I can't believe we got a parking spot," Alana said with a laugh as she got out.

"Must be a sign of good luck coming our way," Jeremy said.

Sarah bounced from the front door and hugged her father first, followed by her soon-to-be stepmother. Alana searched Sarah's face for some indication that Sarah had learned about Alana's failed attempt at acting but found nothing. She hoped that meant nobody would ever tell Sarah that Sarah would be allowed to play the role of Martha without guilt weighing her down.

"Let's get bagels," Sarah said, tugging them along and gushing about that week of "horrible but incredible" rehearsals leading up to today's show. "And Pete already wants me to start learning my lines for the next play!"

"You don't look frantic," Jeremy pointed out. "But I would be."

Sarah smiled and caught Alana's eye. "I just wish you were around to run lines with me. I'm pretty sure you're the only reason any of this happened."

"That's not true," Alana countered, "and you know it. It was pure talent."

Even still, Alana's heart was warm as they floated through the streets and ambled into her and Sarah's favorite bagel place. Jeremy wasn't familiar with it, so they recommended their favorite flavors and cream cheeses and ordered big coffees. They sat outside at a picnic table and watched the early afternoon city dwellers, all of whom seemed up on the latest fashions the latest ways to wear their hair and makeup. Alana felt woefully behind. It reminded her of her years in Paris when she'd realized that fashion had shifted off its axis the slightest bit, and she had to buy an entire new wardrobe. But now that she was an islander, practicality was slowly taking over her life. That, and her love for Jeremy. When you loved someone that much, when they loved you—it meant you just didn't care about the little details as much anymore. Recently, she realized she'd gained a few pounds, but because her wedding dress still fit like a glove, she waved it off. It was no big deal. By comparison, if she'd been an actress preparing for the stage, she would have absolutely panicked.

After bagels, Sarah sped off to prep for the big night ahead. This left Jeremy and Alana to their own devices before the seven-p.m. curtain. They wandered in and out of shops, looked in bookstores for summer reads, and again squabbled gently about where they might go for their honeymoon. They'd decided to wait until October or November when the island was grim and wet and cold. They wanted to squeeze this Nantucket dry of family parties and laughter on the beaches they loved the most.

Alana and Jeremy got ready for the performance at the hotel that had served as Alana's second home for June. The receptionist greeted her like an old friend. "It's been a while! We've missed you."

Alana wasn't sure if she'd missed this wildlife in the city. She'd genuinely adored the previous few weeks of calm, of walking around downtown with an ice cream cone, of trying out new recipes with Jeremy and calling themselves "empty nesters" even though, really, Alana had hardly officially lived with Sarah at all. There had also been final preparations to make for the wedding, which she, Ella, Julia, and their mother had done together. Everything was falling into place. Every detail was accounted for.

Alana changed into a dark red dress that showed a little more leg than a normal forty-seven-year-old might have, but she didn't mind. That was who she was, and she didn't want to feel sorry for it. Jeremy wore a suit that made him look extremely handsome, but the look on his face gave away his nerves. Alana kissed him with her eyes closed and tried to translate to him just how wonderful he looked, but he said, "I'm just a washed-up football player from a little island. I work in a basement and look at records all day." Alana laughed and swatted him. "All the women in that theater won't be able to keep their eyes off you."

It turned out that Alana was mostly right about that. When they entered the foyer, multiple women turned to assess the beautiful couple. Their eyes turned from Jeremy to Alana and back again. They smirked like the models Alana had once known back in her twenties, models who'd wanted Alana's career. But Alana's smile was serene. She understood that what she had was something special; she also knew it wasn't just surface-deep.

"Alana!" Julia called from the opposite end of the foyer, where she stood with the rest of their family. Their father was wearing the brand-new suit he'd gotten for the press tour for his most recent novel, and he looked dapper, like a Cambridge University professor. Alana and Jeremy went around hugging everyone until an usher announced it was time to go in. Alana slipped her hand into Jeremy's and followed him down the aisle to the fourth row, where Sarah had reserved seats for the two of them. The other Copperfields were seated a bit further away but with excellent angles on the action.

The curtain came up to reveal the set that had a downtown street with a casino, a club and an old-world bar, plus shadows of horses and people in the background, as though it was a crowded time in a forgotten era. Alana gripped Jeremy's hand as Sarah made her big entrance. The line was something Sarah had practiced hundreds if not thousands of times back in Nantucket: "It's one thing to be deceived. But to be so heinously directed in a direction that seems wholly alien is another thing entirely! I will never forget that man for the rest of my life. I hate him."

The audience laughed. Sarah had said it perfectly. She'd already won over her audience. For a little while, as the play went on, Alana allowed herself to fall into the magic of the play. She allowed herself to forget that that young woman up there was her darling Sarah. She was a character in this play; she was messy and entirely un-Sarah-like. Once, when Alana glanced over at Jeremy, she caught him crying. His cheeks were gleaming with tears. She squeezed his hand harder, enraptured with him and his sensitivity and the power of his love.

"That's my little girl," he said when it was over. "I can't believe it. She did it."

"She really did," Alana said.

# Chapter Twenty

This was Greta's third wedding in less than a year. You would have thought she would have a handle over her emotions by now, that she wouldn't wake up crying and rush to the bathroom to give herself a pep talk. "These are happy days," she reminded herself as she ran the water and blubbered. "These are the days that remind you just how good it is to be alive."

Greta brewed coffee downstairs and retreated to her study that morning. She'd agreed to host all of the Copperfield women starting at eleven o'clock sharp—with croissants and fresh fruit and cream and Scarlet's famous mimosas, but first, she wanted to write for a few minutes. She wanted to drop back into Celeste's world.

Greta wrote *I've learned bits and pieces about Celeste's wedding to Greg from phone conversations with Greg himself. He was all over the place after our first meeting and initially told me he wasn't sure he was up to talking to me again. But he called me out of the blue in mid-July and said, "I want to tell you as much as you want to know. I want Celeste's life to be recorded. Even the parts she didn't let me know." And so he told me, on the morning of their wedding, Celeste came to find him at his brother's house and told him she couldn't go through with it. She said she was sorry. Greg begged her to help him understand. She said she would if he promised to leave her alone. "Obviously, I was broken-hearted," Greg told me on the phone. "I was completely in love with her, and I'd fallen for those two kids, too. I wanted to build a family with her. But I'll never forget what she said. She said, 'It's all meaningless, Greg. All of it. Love. Life. I don't know if I have the energy for any of it. I don't understand what's happened or what will happen next, and I'm terrified. I'm terrified I'll let you down, or you'll let me down, or we'll fall apart for no reason at all.' I'd never heard her talk like that, but it makes sense, based on what you told me, Greta, that she was a writer of fiction. That she had the heart of an artist. She was so upset. So I took her hand and said, 'All I know is I love you. We can take this one day at a time. And there's no way we'll break each other's hearts. We trust each other completely. And we'll never lie.' I really said that! And meanwhile, she'd never told me anything pertinent about her past. But she told me, 'I want to be true and good to you for the rest of my life.' And I genuinely believe she was. I believe we both woke up every morning and made decisions that made the difficult parts of reality easier for both of us. And I hate so much that she had to leave this planet so early. But I hope I made things comfortable before she had to go."*

Greta wept as she typed and cleaned herself up in the shower just in time for the girls to arrive. Alana was first. She wore a pair of shorts and a tank top and carried her wedding gown in its big plastic bag. "Uh oh," Alana said before she hugged her, "It looks like you've been writing this morning?"

"Are my eyes still red?" Greta sighed and took Alana's wedding dress from her just as Julia and Ella pulled into the driveway. "How are you feeling, honey?"

"I'm wonderful," Alana said. She sounded mystical as she floated into the living room and sat down. The light beamed in from the window and cast her in a glow. "I hope you're okay. Is the book taking too much out of you?"

Greta huffed. "You know how I am with writing. It has to take everything from me. That's the only way I know how to do it."

Julia walked in as she spoke and laughed. "You sound just like all of my writers." She hugged her and added, "But you're much better than they are, Mom. I would beg you to publish with me, but I know you have the Big Five publishing houses chasing after you." There was no ill will behind what Julia said, and Greta smiled. She'd promised to publish a novella with Julia for next year—a short fiction piece about an older woman who handled the dramatic goings-on at an artist residency. She had plenty of inspiration after the past year or so of taking on artists. The list of crazy happenings was a mile long at this point.

The other Copperfield women and Sarah arrived soon afterward, and chaos reigned. Scarlet bopped around, passing out mimosas as Ivy passed out croissants with cream and sliced strawberries that tasted so tart and decadent that it was hard to believe Greta had picked them from a berry bush on that very island. Makeup artists and hairstylists arrived to do everyone's hair, and Laura and Ella took over the LPs, spinning record after record to get Alana and the others in wedding mode, everything from Taylor Swift to David Bowie to Lana Del Ray to The Beatles. Greta fell from one conversation to another and insisted on having "very minimal makeup and very minimal haircare." She just couldn't stand to have too much crap on her face. And being surrounded by the love of her family made her feel beautiful anyway.

The wedding was set to begin at four-thirty that afternoon. A little after twelve-thirty, a crew came by to set everything up, including the floral archway beneath which Alana and Jeremy would say their vows, enough white chairs for the limited number of guests, a speaker system and tables for the heaps of food. Greta was thrilled that somebody else was going to cook for a change, but she had insisted on approving the catering beforehand. She wouldn't have any shoddy food at her daughter's wedding.

Alana put on her wedding dress a few minutes before four, and the Copperfield women went quiet with surprise. Alana was always a beauty queen regardless of what she wore, but the white dress had a startling effect. With her dark hair and dark eyebrows, she looked like a snow queen. Greta felt her eyes fill again. "You look beautiful, honey," she said as everyone remembered they could speak and cried out their agreement.

The men were already here. They required no makeup, just a spritz of cologne and a bit of gel in their hair, and they were off. But when Greta stepped out on the back porch to see them all together, chatting in their suits and tuxedos, her heart skipped a beat. Bernard was standing near Julia's husband, Charlie, smiling and chatting about something or other. It was probably about Charlie's woodworking, which Bernard adored. Charlie had even made Alana and Jeremy a beautiful wooden chest for their wedding, which was a surprise that Greta had nearly spilled the details of to Alana a few weeks ago. She'd been able to clear her tracks. It was close.

Although Alana hadn't opted for traditional bridesmaids, Julia, Ella, Sarah, and Greta served as her official "wedding attendees." They hung back as the others found white chairs on the sand and then walked down the aisle slowly as the string quintet played "Pachelbel's Canon." Greta went last, following behind Julia. She looked every single guest in the eye and remembered how much she loved them and how much they loved Alana and Jeremy. And then she thought about Celeste on her wedding day, frightened out of her mind that something was about to go wrong. That the horrors from her past would come up and bite her. That they would hurt her children or Greg. But Greg had assured her everything would be okay. And wasn't that what marriage was? Bernard was Greta's intellectual equal. She loved his mind and his creativity. But more than that, she loved his heart. She loved his laughter. She loved cuddling up to him in bed and telling him little stories from her day. She loved drinking coffee with him. She loved that when he dunked himself in the ocean, he would always come up and shake his long hair like a scraggly dog. She loved him. And there was very little art in this world that could fully encapsulate what it meant to be in love with someone. Maybe that was what Celeste had figured out when she stepped away from art and writing. Maybe she reached total enlightenment in the form of making sandwiches for her children, flicking around on television and drinking coffee with Greg. Maybe she loved the ability to breathe more than the ability to think and think and think.

Greta held Bernard's hand as Alana came down the

aisle. Her eyes shimmered with the afternoon light, and Jeremy let a single tear fall. He took Alana's hands in his as the pastor raised his hands and said a brief prayer over the couple.

Jeremy went first, "You came back into my life and flipped my world upside down. I had no idea what was in store for me and for us. But every single day has been an adventure ever since. I know who I want to laugh with and cry with, who I want to talk to every morning, and who I want to go to sleep beside every night. I know who I want to sing songs with in the car. And more than that, I know who will uphold my daughter and her life and her choices above everything. The fact that you've taken such good care of Sarah and me since you came into the picture floors me. I love you, Alana. I'm so grateful you want to be my wife."

Alana went next, "I think it's sometimes hard not to have regrets about the past, especially when you've been alive as long as we have." The audience laughed gently. "But I can honestly say that I come to you today on this beautiful day in late July without a single regret. I know that every step we've made, both together and apart since birth, has led us here. I know it was written in the stars that we would grow old together in Nantucket, that all of our past sorrows would fade away in the immensity of our love. I can't wait to talk about this day forever. And I can't wait until we stop fighting about where we're going to go on our honeymoon and just book a flight already. But know that I'm grateful I've found somebody I can fight with. Somebody who takes me seriously. Somebody who holds me when I cry." Alana's voice broke. "I know not everyone is lucky enough to find their person. I will spend the rest of my days thanking my lucky stars I found you again."

Greta and Bernard clutched one another's hands as Alana and Jeremy shared a kiss and sealed their marriage. The Copperfield Family burst up from the sand with applause. There, they stood together in exultation just fifteen feet from The Copperfield House as a big orange sun dropped lower in the afternoon sky and cast long shadows. Very soon, the summer would end and beckon autumn, chilly mornings, and gray dust. But today was for celebration. Today was for champagne and kisses and long nights of dancing. Greta planned to enjoy every minute.

* * *

Coming Next in the Nantucket Sunset Series<br>Pre Order Nantucket Heart

# Other Books by Katie